Bird Brain

A Polly Parrett Pet-Sitter Cozy Murder Mystery
Book 3

Liz Dodwell

Bird Brain: A Polly Parrett Pet-Sitter Cozy Murder Mystery:
Book 3
Copyright © 2016 by Liz Dodwell
www.lizdodwell.com

Published by Mix Books, LLC

Table of Contents

One

"You must be joking!"

"I assure you, Miss Parrett, I don't joke."

Looking at the impassive countenance of Newton Alden, Esquire, I believed him.

We were seated across from each other at Alden's desk. A couple of days earlier I'd received an urgent written request from the firm of Shilito, Draper, Crouch and Alden, Attorneys at Law, to contact them regarding a legal matter. Honestly, my first reaction was that it was a spam letter. I tore it in half, crumpled up the pieces and tossed them in the trash. Of course, Amber immediately pounced, knocking over the trash can with all its contents, and started batting the pieces of paper around the floor as if they were the greatest cat toys ever.

I didn't think anything more of it until later in the day when the phone rang. Assuming it might be a client I answered in my perky voice, "Pets and People, Too. This is Polly, can I help a pet or a person today?"

"My name is Sadie, I'm calling on behalf of Newton Alden, Esquire. Am I speaking with Miss Pauline Parrett?"

I almost said she must have the wrong number. Pauline is my given name but nobody calls me that. I've gone by Polly for as long as I can remember. Then it hit me: Newton Alden, Esquire, the name on the letter I'd shredded earlier.

"This is Pauline, but please call me Polly."

"Miss Parrett," so much for that, "you should have received a letter from Mr. Alden. I'm calling to see if we can arrange a time for you to meet."

"What is this about?" My scam meter was still running.

"You have been named a beneficiary in an estate and Mr. Alden would like to discuss disbursement of the assets as soon as possible."

What? "Who died?"

"The lady's name is Naomi Ledbetter."

"I don't know anybody with that name. Why would she leave anything to me? This must be some mistake."

"There's no mistake, Miss Parrett. I'm sure Mr. Alden will explain everything when you come in."

Well, I was too curious to ignore the summons, so said I could come in the following week. Sadie would have none of that and insisted it would be too late but, when I asked why, she just gave me the runaround. Finally, I gave up and settled on a time the next day. It was really inconvenient for me as I was preparing to exhibit at a pet show over the weekend. I couldn't deny, though, I was a little excited about my mystery benefactor, so I crawled around on the floor looking for the letter. I found half or it under the credenza along with a dozen or so hair-covered glitter poms, a plastic pen top and a tampon wrapper. The second half remained elusive until I headed into the kitchen for another cup of coffee and noticed something in the pets' water dish. Yep! It was the letter, pretty much disintegrated. Sighing, I dumped the water, cleaned out the dish and accepted I'd learn nothing until my meeting.

Now here I was with Newton Alden, Esquire, wondering what on earth I was getting myself into.

"Why me?"

"Miss Ledbetter had you thoroughly vetted and believed you to be the ideal person to take care of this."

"I was investigated?" That sucked a lemon. "That's a bit much."

Alden pursed thin, dry lips. "A person could simply read your facebook page and know more about you than they want to, including your opinion that Bugs Bunny is the greatest cartoon character of all time." He had a point there.

"What if I refuse to take it, whatever it is?"

The man tilted his head back and peered down his nose at me. He had a slight gap between his front teeth and when he spoke it was with a faint, and irritating, whistling noise. "Against my advice, Miss Ledbetter refused to include any provisional arrangements, which means it would become a matter for the court."

For pity's sake. "I suppose I could take a look then."

With no hesitation, Alden hit the intercom button. "Would you come in please, Sadie?"

Just as quickly, the assistant entered. "Yes, sir?"

"Miss Parrett would like to see her bequest now."

"Of course, would you come this way, Miss Parrett?"

"It's here?" I wasn't expecting that but I obediently trotted after Sadie 'til she reached the ladies' room and walked right in.

"Um, I'll just wait for you out here," I said.

"No, this is where we've been keeping it." *Whaaat?*

I pushed past her and found myself facing a blue and gold macaw sitting atop a stainless steel perch to which one leg was chained. These striking birds have vivid blue plumage with a yellow or butterscotch underside and green on top of the head, but this one was a sorry specimen. Macaws are among the most sociable of birds but the poor animal had its head down and was absorbed in plucking at its pin feathers and had created a large bald patch on its chest. The feathers had none of the usual healthy iridescent sheen you should expect to see and, though I'm no expert, to me the creature looked much too thin.

Appalled, I looked around. There was no window, the bird had no toys, no distractions of any kind, only food pellets to eat and, obviously, no company. I reached out to stroke the macaw's head and it promptly bit me, drawing blood.

"Oh, it does that," Sadie said. "It's not very nice."

"Nice!" I seethed. "If I'd been shoved in here like this I'd be ready to claw your eyes out. How long has he been in here?"

When Sadie didn't respond I spun round and marched back to Alden's office, flinging open the door. "I'll take it, you miserable, mean man. You should be ashamed of what you've done to that poor bird. And that goes for you, too," I said, glaring at the assistant who'd been dogging my footsteps.

"We did the best we could," she snapped. "This isn't a zoo."

"Really? Then how come I'm in a room with an ass and an ape?"

"That's enough." Alden, eternally impassive, whistled through his teeth. "Sadie, put the bird in its cage and get it ready for Miss Parrett to take."

"Me? But it will bite. I can't..."

"Just find a way, Sadie." Then to me he said, "And we have some other business to conclude before you leave, Miss Parrett."

I gave him my most contemptuous look. "I have nothing more to say."

"There is more to the bequest, which I think you will find quite agreeable."

Oh, lord. Not more birds. I sat.

"Miss Ledbetter added a clause to her will. It is conditional on your acceptance of her pet's welfare for the rest of its life. You will receive the balance of Miss Ledbetter's estate, after legal fees and expenses have been satisfied, of course."

Well, I wasn't expecting that. "Um...uh, I...I'm not sure I understand."

"Having agreed to care for Polly, you will receive..."

"Whoa, hold up just a minute. Polly? The parrot's name is Polly?"

For the first time, Alden looked a little uncomfortable. "I believe your name was part of the reason Miss Ledbetter chose you as her beneficiary."

"This just gets better and better." I flung my hands up. "Polly Parrett and Polly Parrot. What a farce. Miss L must have had quite the sense of humor."

Alden cleared his throat. "As I was saying, you are also the recipient of a residential home with all contents, valued at $94,000. There is a certificate of deposit and a bank account with a combined total of $4,058. Fees will be in the region of $3,000 to $4,000. Probate should be quite straightforward. The estate is small and I've handled Miss Ledbetter's affairs for many years, so I anticipate we will be able to wrap this up within no more than ninety days."

I couldn't speak. I'd pretty much stopped listening at $94,000. To me that was a fortune. Alden rattled on about probates and appraisals and such, then handed me forms that I signed in a daze. He had Sadie make copies and the next thing I was really aware of was standing outside the offices of Messrs. Shilito, Draper, Crouch and Alden with a bird in a cage in one hand, a wad of papers in the other and a bunch of bird paraphernalia beside me.

My van was parked on the street so I shuttled everything to it. Moving any bird is incredibly stressful for them and this one was already a mess. Thankfully, I always keep a spare cat carrier or five with me and, using a towel, I carefully extricated Polly from her cage and secured her in the carrier. By now, she was so traumatized, she didn't even object.

It was an easy decision to head to my mother's rather than my own home. There were people there who could help and Polly Parrot desperately needed help. "Hang in there, pretty girl," I crooned. "Everything will be alright." But would it?

Two

The weekend

The poodle, a standard white, was wearing a princess costume with a tiara on her head. By her side, a little toy poodle, black, was dressed up to look like a frog prince. At their owner's command, both dogs stood on their hind legs and paraded across the field. The crowd roared approval.

"It's amazing the lengths people will go to for a fancy dress dog contest," Tina said.

We were both standing on our chairs watching the action. It was the second annual state pet-sitters association jamboree. Vendors' booths were arranged in a circle facing each other across the open field where all the activities took place – agility contests, demonstrations, fancy dress contest – and attendees milled around, browsing the merchandise and watching the shows.

The little town of Mallowapple, where I live, had been chosen as the site for the event, mostly because it was fairly central in the state. Proceeds went to charity. This year, a group had been chosen that rescued shelter dogs and trained them as service dogs for military veterans. It was something dear to my heart because my mother and I had conceived and were running our own 501c for homeless vets and their pets. Well, actually Mom did pretty much everything.

I probably should back up a bit and explain.

A couple of Christmases ago I got involved in a murder where a homeless Vietnam veteran and his dog were wrongly accused of murder. Happily, they were exonerated and when my mom met Rooster, the ex-army guy, and his pit bull, Elaine, she came up with the idea to turn her big old farmhouse into a sort of half-way house for homeless vets and their pets.

Rooster had moved in and between the three of us – and any other volunteers we could find – we'd fixed up the place and waded through mountains of paperwork to apply for non-tax status, which I can tell you is a major headache. We'd decided on a simple name: Welcome Home. Members of the local VFW (Veterans of Foreign Wars) had provided legal and accounting assistance free of charge and my brother, Seb, who was the techie of the family, set up a website.

Our attorney, an ex-navy man named Orvil Gilroy, instructed we should have an advisory board even though we intended to keep our charity local, and preferably, someone with fund-raising experience. Callisto Padovano, known as Cal, a retired CPA, recommended we develop a five-year budget and operating plan and begin the fund-raising efforts immediately.

So, here I was at the jamboree with a booth to promote my pet-care business and raise awareness for Welcome Home. In a wave of optimism I'd printed a bunch of flyers explaining what Welcome Home was about, and had set a big glass fishbowl on the table hoping for a few donations. Surprisingly, people had been quite generous and I was happily anticipating the look on Mom's face when I handed her the loot.

"Polly, look at this one." Tina, who is part of my pet-sitting crew, yanked my sleeve. I turned as the announcer's voice came over the speakers. "And here is Yogi."

Yogi, a cute little bichon frise, was masquerading as a racehorse with a stuffed jockey on his back, while his guardian, Sherry, who also happened to be a client, paraded him in front of the crowd. I waved at her and cheered for Yogi when a blur of movement right in front of me drew my attention. Stunned, I realized someone had snatched up my donation jar and was racing off behind the booth.

"Stop thief," I shrieked, thrusting myself from the folding chair, which promptly collapsed, dumping me face first onto the ground that was still muddy from an early morning shower. Helplessly, I watched as my precious funds were carried away. Fudge!

Then from the line of vendor booths a dog appeared, running toward the thief with long, effortless strides. In seconds he closed the gap and as he reached the thief, lunged at him, grabbing hold of the man's arm. The thief howled and jerked to a halt but managed to maintain his footing, at the same time swinging his other arm back with the jar in hand. *He's going to smash the dog's head.*

I think I stopped breathing, then I heard a forceful voice. "Aus!" Instantly the dog released his hold and backed away, which caused the guy to lose his footing and his hold on my money. Down they went. The thief stayed in one piece but the jar shattered and a light breeze began to gently carry the bills away.

I thought I heard someone yell "giblets," though what chicken parts had to do with anything was beyond me, and by now I was more focused on the fact that a horde of people had realized what was happening and converged on the area, snatching at the loose money. Hauling myself to my feet I hobbled toward the activity trying to snag a stray dollar or two along the way.

My knee was throbbing like crazy, which was really a pity because I wanted to kick the scumbag thief in the you-know-whats. How could anyone steal from people in need?

The dog was standing over the thief, barking like crazy. He was a powerful-looking German shepherd, black and tan with dark muzzle and dark ears. As I got close, he broke away and heeled beautifully next to a muscular-looking guy with a high and tight haircut. Someone caught hold of my arm; it was one of the event organizers, Tom, I think. "Security is on the way," he said, and I watched as they arrived, seized the robber and marched him away.

In moments, the whole thing was over. The crowd had dispersed along with the money; even the dog and his master were nowhere in sight. I wanted to cry but that would make me look like a wuss and I still had a little pride, so instead, I limped back to my booth.

Three

How quickly moods can change. The day had begun with so much promise. For a May day in Maine it was expected to be sunny and in the 60s. I'd splurged and bought one of those pop-up canopies and had a banner made with my company name, Pets and People, Too, which was strung above the table where my information and give-a-ways were displayed. To make the set-up even more appealing I'd had the brilliant idea to create a backdrop using a photo of all my own "fur-kids." OK, it really wasn't such a brilliant idea; the using my kids part, anyway. After two hours of trying to get my three dogs and six cats to pose prettily together, I gave up and bought a stock picture where all the animals looked perfect.

Now, all I could focus on was the empty space where my jar had been.

"Here," Tina said, "sit down."

She drew me towards a chair but I glared at it suspiciously. "Is that the one that tossed me?"

"It's fine." She shook it to prove the point and it seemed reasonably stable, so I sat, wincing as my knee bent.

"You need to get that iced," Tina said. "I'm going over to the medical tent to see if they can help. Will you be OK for a few minutes?"

"I think I'd feel much better if you would stop at the ice-cream van and bring me a double dip of pistachio." I gave my best "pitiful me" impression and Tina headed off, shaking her head.

"Polly!" It was Tom, or whatever his name was. I really should try harder to remember people's names. Pets are easy; people – not so much.

"Hey, uh, you." Well, what else was I going to say?

"I think we rounded up most of it, and we're going to make an announcement before the next event begins."

"Huh?" Not the most astute comment, I grant you, but I had no idea what he was talking about.

"I didn't have another jar to put it in, so I had to make do with a bag." He held out a white plastic bag with the words, "Thank You" printed in red on the side. "Well go on. Take it!"

Uncertainly, I took the bag and sat it on my lap then peered inside. Holy cow. For once I didn't know what to say. The bag was full of money. Mostly one dollar bills, some fives, and here and there a ten and even twenty. "But, I...."

"Some people added a little extra when they found out what it was for. We're all really impressed with what you and your family are doing for needy military vets. And their pets, of course. Anyway, I must dash, it's almost time for Tootsie and her Dancing Dog to do their number."

"Wait. How can I thank everybody for their generosity? This is so wonderful."

"I'll pass along your words, but the best thanks would be to keep doing what you're already doing. Make us proud, Polly."

What was I saying earlier about moods changing quickly? 'Cause right now, I was on top of the world. "I'll certainly do my best," I said. "Oh, one more thing. Who is the guy with the German shepherd who brought the thief down? I really want to talk to him in person."

"You'll find him at the K9 Security booth. Now I really must go."

Whatshisname took off at a swift pace leaving me to contemplate the kindness of my fellow man, and woman, of course. Tina returned with an ice pack and ice cream, which boosted my good humor even more. And a little later, when I tried to stand, the pain in my knee had reduced to a dull ache.

"I'm going to see if I can find the guy with the dog," I announced to Tina. "Can you hold down the fort?"

We'd been doing some brisk business; signed on several new clients and gathered a bunch of leads. Meanwhile, donations had been pouring in along with offers to help with Welcome Home. Now the show was winding down and I was looking forward to getting home, but I really wanted to thank the hero and his dog.

"No problem," Tina said.

I found K9 Security just a few booths away but it was empty. There were stacks of leaflets on the table so I picked one up and read:

K9 SECURITY GUARD DOG SERVICES
Effective
Dependable
Inexpensive

Underneath was a picture of a snarling shepherd.

"Hi, there. Can we help you?"

Startled, I turned to see two of the most hunky guys I'd ever dreamed of. It was obvious they both spent a lot of time in the gym by the way their t-shirts were stretched tight over their torsos. At heel next to them were two German shepherds.

"Hey, you must be the gal who had her money stolen. We were told it was someone from Pets and People, Too."

I must have looked blank because the one who spoke nodded at my breasts. I looked down. Oh, right. My logo was embroidered on the polo shirt I was wearing. Awkward.

"Um, yes. I'm Polly Parrett." I held out my hand.

A large hand covered mine but its owner was careful not to give a crushing shake.

"Mat Abaroa, and this is my partner, Jake Sinasohn."

In his turn Jake shook hands, then after the formal introductions were over I looked at the dogs. "And who are these guys?"

"Larry and Moe."

I laughed. "Don't tell me there's a Curly somewhere?"

Both men grinned and Jake replied. "As a matter of fact, we're training Curly right now."

For those of you who don't know, Larry, Moe and Curly were the names of The Three Stooges, a trio of vaudeville players famous for their slapstick comedy routines in the mid-1900s.

"Listen," I got serious, "I really want to thank whichever one of you saved my day."

"That would be Mat and Larry." Jake cocked his head toward his partner.

"It's all in a day's work for us," Mat said, "And good practice for Larry."

"Can I pet him?"

"Sure."

I gave the dog a good scruff behind the ears. "You're a really good boy."

Larry slowly waved his tail and gave me a happy dog grin.

I chatted with the guys for a little while, asking about their business and training methods. Jake explained they used German commands. Turned out he was of German origin as well; his first name was actually Jakob.

"That explains why I didn't understand the commands you used," I said to Mat. "But what was it that sounded like 'giblets?' "

The men looked at each with raised eyebrows, then understanding dawned and they burst out laughing.

"That was 'Gib Laut.' It's the command for bark."

I laughed as well, though a little self-consciously, then figured it was time to take my leave.

"I'm going to take some of your leaflets to hand out and if I can ever help you guys, let me know. It seems so inadequate to just say thanks."

"We'll take a hug and call it quits," Jake said and he put his arms round me and gave a squeeze. When Mat grabbed me he lifted me off my feet. All that manhood was making me a little giddy and I laughed self-consciously, which was when I heard a voice say, "Hello, Polly."

It was Tyler – my boyfriend.

Four

"They're really good guys," Tyler said. He was referring to Mat and Jake. We were in my van on the way to Welcome Home. Tyler had insisted on driving when he saw the state of my knee. I'd used the drive time to tell him everything that had happened. He just might be the most amazing guy ever. Not only was he totally caring and concerned about me, he wasn't at all bothered when he found me in the embrace of another guy. Just a minute, maybe I should be pissed he wasn't jealous.

"So it doesn't bother you if other men find me attractive?"

"Certainly not when they're gay."

I felt heat begin to rise in my face and knew it must be turning red as Tyler glanced over at me.

"Seriously?" He grinned. "You didn't know?"

"They said they were partners. I figured they just meant business partners." I was feeling a bit defensive, and let down. I'd never been confident about my looks so I'd been enjoying the thought that a couple of great-looking guys might think I was cute. Tyler read my thoughts immediately, though.

"Oh, honey, guys look at you all the time. Believe me, I've seen them, and it makes me proud that you're with me." Wow. I am one lucky lady to have this guy.

Changing the subject, Tyler continued. "You've had quite an exciting few days. Now you'll have to decide what to do about your inheritance."

"You're going to help me deal with the house." Tyler's a realtor; I looked pointedly at him. "As for my alter ego, Polly Parrot, apparently the new guy has taken charge of her."

We had taken in a new resident very recently. He didn't arrive with a pet but Welcome Home wasn't going to exclude any veteran who needed housing; it's just that we would also welcome their pets when they had them, while most shelters would not.

"What do you know about him?"

"His name's Mike something, he lost a leg in Iraq, though he seems to do well with his prosthetic, and that's about it. I only met him briefly last week."

"Well, I guess I can find out for myself," Tyler said as we pulled up in front of the old homestead.

The dogs must have alerted the household to our arrival. The front door opened and my three, Angel, Vinny and Coco, burst through, followed by an equally happy, though less bouncy, Elaine. You know, one of the greatest things in the world is to be greeted by a dog. It's as if you just made her whole life worth living.

Rooster and Mike came out to help Tyler unload my stuff. There wasn't space to store it at my little house in town so the huge basement in the farmhouse was a blessing. As the men worked I limped inside and found Mom in the kitchen. She spun her wheelchair and smiled.

"I thought you'd probably be hungry by the time you got here. There's oxtail stew ready to go and I made a lemon meringue pie."

I gazed fondly at my mother. A couple of years ago she'd been a bitter, miserable woman. A horse-riding accident had crippled her, and her constant, self-indulgent pity had driven my dad away. But the Welcome Home project had brought back the vital, resourceful woman I loved. Her wheelchair was no longer a handicap but a tool she used to great effect. And since Rooster had been in residence he'd made a lot of improvements for Mom. In the kitchen, countertops had been lowered, cupboards now had pull-out and drop-down shelves, the microwave was at chair height and both the stove top and sink were open underneath so Mom could wheel right up. It was brilliant.

Between us Mom and I set the table, by which time the men were done and we all sat. With the exception of Rooster, the residents usually cooked for themselves in the kitchen of the converted barn. Tonight, though, Mike was joining us at the house to update us on the macaw's condition.

It was an enjoyable meal. Once again I recounted my story and Rooster told us he'd counted the donations and we had more than three hundred dollars! We discussed what to do about the house I now owned. Mom wanted me to keep the inheritance for myself; I argued it would be better used toward rehabbing the farm property for Welcome Home. Finally, Tyler stepped in and suggested we assess the house first, then make a decision, and we all agreed that was best.

"So, Mike. How's Po..." I just couldn't quite bring myself to say the name. "How's the bird?"

The young man had barely spoken throughout the meal. When I addressed him he visibly tensed and snatched at his glass, sloshing water on the table. His eyes dilated and he dropped his chin to his chest, mumbling rapid apologies. Taken aback, I looked helplessly at him 'til Rooster, the seasoned veteran, put out a calming hand and squeezed his shoulder.

"It's alright, son. You're with friends. Nobody minds a little spill. Why don't you tell Polly what you were telling me earlier, about why you think the parrot's been pulling its feathers out?"

Mike looked up and Rooster gave him an encouraging nod. He turned to me, though didn't quite make eye contact and spoke haltingly.

"She's depressed. And frightened. And lonely."

That didn't surprise me, and I told Mike how the macaw had been kept in the bathroom after her owner died. As I talked, he began to relax and paid close attention to my words, nodding in understanding.

"Parrots are very sociable; they like company. Polly, uh, that's the parrot not, uh...you..."

"I get it, Mike. Go on."

"Well, she would have been very attached to the old lady. Imagine if your Mom died and then you were shut away in a bathroom for days or weeks with no company and nothing to do."

"Uh, yes," I said, because I just didn't know how else to respond.

Rooster leaned forward resting his arms on the table. "Mike has already developed a bond with the macaw, haven't you son? Tell us what you do to help her."

"I talk to her. At first she didn't listen but after a while she started to pay attention, especially when I told her we are from the same part of the world, and I described the beautiful rainforests with their colorful fruits and flowers."

"What part of the world is that, Mike?" Tyler asked.

"I was born in Colombia, but my family came here to America soon after. That's why I am called Mike. They wanted me to be American, to have an American name. I am Mike Martinez."

"And where are your family?"

It seemed a natural enough question for Mom to ask, but it had a bizarre effect on Mike who shot to his feet. "I have to go." And he rushed from the room leaving us all wondering what had just happened. Well, all of us but Rooster.

"He lost a leg to an IED in Iraq. Worse still, he lost his best friend in the blast."

"Survivor's guilt?" Tyler asked.

"I'm sure, and PTSD. He needs help but he's resisting it. I had a hard time persuading him to stay at Welcome Home so I don't want to push too hard. Believe it or not, tonight was progress. It was a big step for him to sit at a table with a group of near strangers and actually make conversation."

"But what about his family?" I asked. "Surely they can help."

"He hasn't spoken of them and, like I said, it's best not to push. We don't even know how he found us. He turned up at the door and asked if there was any work he could do in exchange for a bed for a night. Turns out he's a pretty fair hand at fixing things so we've got plenty to keep him busy but, until he took charge of your macaw, I had to coax him to spend each day with us."

"He's not dangerous, is he? He's awfully moody and I'd hate to think of Mom being here alone with him."

"Nonsense!" Mom was emphatic. "He's a nice boy who's lived through a really bad time. He needs a place where he feels accepted and that's what Rooster and I intend to give him. Besides, the animals all took to him right away. Cappy was on his lap the first night and even Ollie has been snuggling up to him. And I don't know how we would have coped with Polly without him. The bird has given him purpose; something that needs him and doesn't criticize."

Three of my cats, Cappy and Ollie, along with Leif, live with my mother. Ollie had been mauled as a baby when a neighbor found him and brought him to me. It took months for him to recover, physically that is, but even eight years later he's still very timid, so I was surprised at his rapid acceptance of Mike. The guy must certainly have something going for him. To reinforce that thought, Mike walked back into the room at that moment with Ms. Parrot on his arm. He held his arm close to his chest and the bird sat facing him.

"I thought you might like to see her," he said, and held out his arm to reveal her.

"I'll be a monkey's uncle. She's beginning to look better already." Seriously, I did think she'd gained a wee bit of weight and I swear there was a little glimmer in her eyes.

"Will she bite if I stroke her?"

"I'll tell her it's OK." He put his mouth close to her head and made soft tutting noises while I reached out and ran my fingers over her feathers. She arched her neck and made kissing sounds. I was thrilled.

"Mike, you're a bird whisperer."

He looked shyly pleased. "I've been keeping her in my bedroom and feeding her fresh fruit with her pellets. She really likes grapes. And some of her pin feathers are beginning to grow back in."

I peered at her chest. "Well, so they are." *Who'da thought it?*

"We need to do something about her name, though. It's not going to work having two Polly Parretts - or Parrots - in the house."

"But she's used to that name." *So am I.* Mike's expression was rather plaintive, then an idea seemed to dawn on him. "Do you know how old she is?"

"As a matter of fact, it was on the paperwork I got from the lawyer's office. She's 38."

"And how old are you?"

"Weeell…"

"She's 28," my mother chimed in, trying not to laugh at my discomfort.

"Then it's settled. She's the oldest, she's had the name longest; she should keep it."

There's no arguing with that kind of logic.

Soon after, Tyler and I were heading home. He was going to take the van after dropping me off. In the morning his sister, Suzette, would help him pick up his car, which was still at the site of the jubilee, and bring the van back to me. I was just keeping my fingers crossed there'd be no early morning pet-care emergencies. As things looked right now my morning was open, so Tyler and I planned to take a look at Naomi Ledbetter's house.

When we got to my place, Tyler jumped from the van and escorted me inside with the dogs, then immediately began to check around. I shook my head.

"It's time you stopped doing that. The boogie man is not going to jump out at me."

"As long as I'm here, it doesn't hurt to be sure."

Remember I told you I'd been involved in a murder a couple of Christmases ago? Well, the killer attacked me in my driveway one night. In fact, that's the singular incident that really brought Tyler and me together. Then, the following Christmas, I was involved in another murder. Anyway, because of that, whenever Tyler is at my house he can't help but look for errant criminals. It's rather sweet, really.

"Alright," Tyler said, pulling me to him, "it's time I left."

I wrapped my arms around his neck while Vinny, my bossy miniature poodle, did his damndest to push between us. We ignored him.

"You could stay," I said, causing Tyler to draw in a quick breath, "on the couch."

He groaned. "I can't be that close to you all night and guarantee my behavior."

He didn't know it, but I'm not sure I could guarantee mine, either. It's not that I'm a prude, but as sure as Newton's apple fell to the ground, I was crazy in love with this guy and it was scaring the dickens out of me.

"I'm sorry, Tyler. I'm just not ready…."

"Ready, yet. I know." He sighed. "I can wait. Especially for someone really worth waiting for."

He lowered his head and placed a long, soft kiss on my lips while we gazed into each other's eyes. As he pulled away he gave a rueful grin and abruptly changed the subject. "You know, maybe I'll call you Iris from now on, seeing as Polly Parrot is the winner in the name sweepstakes."

I pulled a face. By calling me Iris he was referring to my heterochromia iridum, which is a fancy way of saying

I have different colored eyes: one iris was brown, the other green.

"You're right," Tyler noted my grimace, "you need an exotic name to match the mystique your eyes give you. I'll have to think about it."

"You do that." And I shoved him out the door.

Five

Stale air enveloped us as we stepped through the front door of my inheritance and into the living room.

"Ewww. Let's leave the door open," I said, "and air the place out a bit."

Tyler flicked the light switch; nothing happened, so I stepped to the window and pulled back the vintage floral drapes. As I turned to see what the light revealed, a scratching noise further inside made me freeze and my heartbeat skipped up a few beats. I looked at Tyler.

"Did you hear that?"

He nodded while putting his finger to his lips. We stood still and silent and there was the noise again.

"What is it?" I hissed.

"Go to the car and lock yourself in while I check it out."

"I'm not going anywhere. There's safety in numbers. Wait! Was that a dog whining?"

Unsure of ourselves we hesitated then tentatively I called out, "Here puppy. Come here."

There was a whining and scrabbling before a brown dog came dashing into the room, all wriggly excitement and nervous apology.

"Oh, you're just a puppy." I dropped to my knees and the delighted youngster rolled onto his back, exposing his belly for me to rub. "You're so thin, you poor boy. How did you get in here?"

"He's with me."

My head snapped up at the sound of a strange voice, while Tyler jumped between me and the man standing in the doorway. "Who the heck are you?"

The man's clothes were garbage chic, like maybe fifty years ago they'd been considered quality. His face was masked behind a scruffy beard and he wore an old cap, which he pulled from his head and twisted nervously in his hands. "I didn't break in. I knocked on the door to ask if there was work I could do and it was open, so I came inside..." His voice trailed off uncertainly and he turned away from us, unable to make eye contact.

"And you expect us to believe that?" Tyler said. "I'm calling the police."

"No, please don't. I didn't mean any harm. I just wanted some food for me and my dog. If you call the police they'll take him away. He's the only friend I've got, please just let us go."

I was having a definite déjà vu moment. Glancing at Tyler it was apparent he was experiencing the same thing. It wasn't so long ago we'd met Rooster and Elaine in an equally bizarre way. Except that this time there wasn't a body. At least, I hope there's no body.

For reassurance I tucked my hand into Tyler's. "Alright, we won't call the cops - yet. But who are you and why should we let you go?"

"Ma'am, I'm Delbert Forlong and this is Jack. We've been on the road together since I found him with his head stuck in a mayonnaise jar. That was back maybe a couple hundred miles ago. I figured he probably had a home nearby but he decided to come along with me instead. I guess I shoulda gone south, but I figured not many of us would come this way and I'd have more chance of work. That hasn't happened. Fact is, it's been real hard."

"You said 'not many of us.' Who'd you mean by that?"

"Well, ma'am, I mean people who don't have a real home to go to every night, so they wander from place to place."

"And why are you on the road?"

Forlong hesitated, nervously running his hands over his thighs before telling his story.

"I was twenty years in the air force, married, with beautiful twin daughters. My wife had been griping for years she'd had enough of the military lifestyle, so I let her persuade me to retire. Problem was, my background in military intelligence didn't relate to anything in the civilian world. My wife's job had been to take care of the home and kids and she didn't think that should change, even though the girls were off to college. And that's another thing, college fees will eat through your savings faster than you can believe.

"So anyways, after a year, there was no money except my pension and whatever I could make odd-jobbing. We couldn't meet the rent. I was forty-four and started smoking to calm my nerves, and the more my wife bitched about that the more I smoked. My girls wouldn't speak to me 'cause it looked like they'd have to drop out of school and they thought I'd let them down. They were right, of course. I had." At this, the sadness emanating from him was almost palpable. It depressed the heck out of me.

"What happened?"

He sighed a deep shaking breath. "My wife went to live with her parents and they took over the college fees for the twins. I'm really grateful to them for that, though they completely shut me out of my girls' lives. My pension goes to them; I just hope they know it.

"For a while I stayed with different friends, 'til I wore the friendship out. Then there was nothing left for me but to hit the road."

Tyler's face was etched with concern as we exchanged glances.

"Look," Forlong went on in a pleading tone, "maybe you've got some work I can do for you. I don't want anything for me, just a meal for Jack. I'll do anything. Just don't take him away."

Jack was leaning against me - you know the way some dogs do – and nudged my hand to remind me it was OK to scratch his ears. At any rate, it made my decision easy.

"Delbert, it's your lucky day."

It was decided that I would zip over to a nearby burger place to get some food (Tyler was still wary enough not to want me to be alone with our new acquaintance) while Delbert helped take room measurements. As I headed out to the car, Jack bounded along beside me.

"No, puppy. You have to stay."

"It's OK," Delbert said. "He's seems to have taken a shine to you."

I'm always happy to be in the company of a dog so I opened the back door of Tyler's Subaru and lifted Jack in. Of course, as soon as I sat in the driver's seat he clawed his way to the front and onto my lap.

"Ah, ah!" Firmly I set him in the passenger seat and gave him "the look," the one that means, "I'm in charge and you'd better stay right there." He wagged his tail happily and did just that. "Well, I'll be. You're a pretty smart little guy." And off we went.

"I'll take a double quarter pounder, plain, and three Big Mac meals with coffee."

"Ju..yun..dream..that?" Huh? I hate these drive-through speaker systems but after several repeat attempts figured out I was being asked if I needed cream for the coffees.

"Better give me a few, please."

I drove round to the pick-up window. Jack could barely contain himself as his nose picked up the scent of grilling beef, and his bony little body was shaking in anticipation. I held out some money as the cashier opened the window. "That was a double Quarter Pounder, three Big Mac meals and three coffees with two creams," she said.

Two creams? "No, I said a few creams."

"Hold on." The woman turned away to grab the order, at which time the excitement was just too much for Jack. He launched himself across my body and through the open windows. The cashier shrieked like a banshee. Whoever was on the receiving end of the speaker probably burst an eardrum. Instinctively I grabbed for Jack and got a hold of his tail so that he ended up with his head and shoulders in the drive-through window, his rear end in the car, and legs scrabbling frantically for leverage to keep going. I was losing my grip on him when a muscular arm reached around the pup's middle and pulled him, squirming, to safety. A voice I recognized said, "Pfui!" and immediately Jack was still.

From a car behind me a voice called out, "Hey, thanks lady. I'll be putting this on youtube," and I saw a cell phone pointed in my direction. Great.

Inside the restaurant the cashier was still in hysterics and being supported by a couple of her co-workers.

"Sorry, sorry," I said before looking up into the laughing face of Mat Abaroa.

"Why don't you pull over so these other people can get their orders." He waved vaguely at the line of cars and curious onlookers building up behind me. Hurriedly, I found a parking space and wondered how much trouble I was in.

The passenger door opened and Mat set Jack down beside me.

"Mat, you must think I'm a terminal idiot. Things just seem to happen to me. Do you think they'll call the police?"

"Lock the dog in the car for just a couple minutes and let's go find out."

He was still grinning and his solid presence helped put me a little at ease, especially when he put his arm round my shoulders. None-the-less, I was pretty worried.

"Why am I not surprised that you have something to do with this?" The woman who spoke had directed her words to Mat and she stood, arms akimbo, hip hiked and head tilted questioningly.

"Hey, Sky, this is Polly Parrett. Polly, meet Skyler Abaroa, who just happens to be my wonderful sister-in-law," and he gave me a sideways wink.

Back at the house – I suppose I should say my house – I related my tale of woe while we ate our food sitting on an ugly old yellow-checked sofa. I'd let Jack have a burger before we left the restaurant parking lot; the pooch was half-starved after all. Unfortunately, there was now a rather ugly grease stain on the car seat – the car that Tyler drove his clients in! I hadn't broken that news to him yet.

"You're sure there won't be any trouble?" Delbert wasn't convinced that Mat had smoothed everything over. In fact, Sky had laughed herself silly about it, commenting she hoped the restaurant would be mentioned in the youtube video. Even the cashier, Maude, once she calmed down went out to meet Jack and pronounced him "Adorable."

"How lucky was it that Mat happened to be there?" Tyler said.

"And that the owners happen to be Mat's brother and sister-in-law."

"We should invite him and Jake out to dinner sometime."

I lifted the corner of my lip in a little smile. "Mat would certainly like that. He did ask me to give his best to 'that really cute boyfriend' of mine."

I wasn't sure, but it looked as if Tyler began to blush. He covered it by jumping up and announcing that it was time we took our new friends to Welcome Home. We'd thoroughly looked over the house and gathered all the information needed, so we piled into the car - me first, plopping my butt on the stain – and joined the traffic heading to Mallowapple.

Six

Several weeks had passed since Delbert, or Del, as he preferred, had taken up residence at Welcome Home. The guys were making progress on converting the second of two old stable buildings to a bunkhouse; Polly (the parrot, that is) was thriving under Mike's care; and Jack had taken to eating the catnip-filled socks I made for the cats. Twice he'd had to be rushed to the vet and Mom was putting pressure on Del to make more effort to train him.

"Honestly, Polly, he's a nice man but he doesn't seem to have much connection with the dog." Through the phone Mom's frustration was evident in her voice. "As for house-training, Jack's definitely all boy and I'm tired of picking up his messes."

"I'm sorry, Mom. I'll talk to Del. That's his responsibility." I'd noticed, too that Jack didn't seem as bonded to Del as I would have expected.

"Something definitely needs to be done before he turns into a complete terror. Can't you spend some time training him?"

"I'll try and get out there more, Mom, but it's Del who really needs training. He's got to learn to be more attentive and consistent. Anyway, enough of that for now, I want to talk to you about the furniture from the house.

"The estate sale company aren't interested in it. They said no-one will buy it because it's so dated and I should just have it hauled away. Tyler got a call from a company who clear out homes for a fee. He said he'd get back to them but they've been pretty aggressive, said they'd waive the fee, and finally even offered to pay him something for the stuff. But here's my thought. How about we use it for the bunkhouse? It's all really solid and I bet with a bit of paint and some fixing up Rooster could work his magic on it."

"That's a great idea, honey, and we can store it in the horse barn for now."

The third barn on the property was a working horse barn, with three rescued horses in residence. Mom gave riding lessons, which she loved, and it brought in enough income to cover the cost of caring for the animals.

Anyway, it was arranged that Rooster, Mike and Del would use a rental truck to pick up everything a couple of days later and transport it to the barn. I'd intended to throw my weight into the mix but, of course, life got in the way and I had to fill in for a crew member with a sick baby and take over her pet sits. Amazingly, the move went well without me (OK, I'm being sarcastic) and, talking to Rooster on the phone the next morning, I was heartened at his enthusiasm for our "treasure."

"You know, the old lady invested in some real quality items. It's a shame people don't appreciate it these days. Some of that furniture will be around long after your grandchildren."

"I'm a long way off from having grandchildren."

"Exactly."

Ignoring the dig I told Rooster I would be at the home in another day or two. "I'm swamped with work right now but you and I should take an inventory of everything as soon as we can. And I promised Mom I'd talk to Del sometime soon."

"Good luck with that. We don't know where he is."

"What do you mean?"

"Jack was barking like crazy in Del's room early this morning. I looked in, thinking something might be wrong, and Del was gone. Looked like his bed hadn't been slept in."

"That's pretty strange."

"Maybe not. For people like us," he meant homeless people, "transitioning to a more normal life, especially with any sort of family, isn't always easy. You get used to open spaces and being alone and sometimes the urge to get away can be really powerful."

"But surely he wouldn't leave Jack?"

"That's one of the things that does puzzle me."

"One of the things! What else is on your mind?"

"Well, he left a pack of smokes on the nightstand. A lot of homeless people smoke; maybe most of them. And though you might think it's crazy to burn money up that way when you can't even afford to eat, the fact is that sometimes a cigarette can seem like your only friend. I can't see Del going off and leaving his smokes."

Now I was feeling a nagging concern. "So Del left both his friends – his dog and his cigarettes. What do you think we should do?"

"Mike and I took a look around the property and I don't think there's anything else we can do just yet except wait. Your mom said if he doesn't show by this evening we'll call the sheriff."

There was really nothing I could add to that and if I didn't get going I'd be late for my first appointment. So we said our farewells and I dashed off to walk a little charmer of a dog, a black and white fluffball named Boo. But I couldn't quite get rid of that troubling feeling in the pit of my stomach.

Seven

Paperwork was strewn across the table. I was immersed in updating the time sheets when the first shot "popped" and something flew by me just nicking my ear. I threw myself to the floor as I heard more popping sounds. Amber streaked past while the dogs all jumped up in excitement at the new game I was playing. "Down," I shrieked, terrified one of them would be seriously hurt.

In moments it was over but I lay still trying to get my mind around what had just happened and to allow my frantically beating heart to slow down. Then something white and squishy plopped onto the floor beside me. I jerked back. Oh my God. Had one of the cats been hit?

I couldn't seem to get my brain to work until I smelled burning and jolted into action. Grabbing the fire extinguisher from its hook in the kitchen I hosed down the torched pan in which I'd been boiling eggs. Oh, boy! This was embarrassing. My intent had been to make deviled eggs for Tyler – one of his favorites – but I'd forgotten the pot was on the range. The popping sound was the eggs exploding as they boiled dry. The detritus of the explosion had been launched around the kitchen and was now stuck to the walls and even the ceiling.

Of course, that was when Tyler walked in. His jaw dropped. The dogs did their best to give him a warm greeting but they were pretty busy eating bits of egg off the floor.

"Deviled eggs," I said in a whisper, and burst into tears.

Realization showed on Tyler's face and he took two quick steps to me and swept me into his arms. I would have felt much better except he couldn't stop laughing.

"Honey, nobody could ever say life is boring around you."

The pizza was delicious. Tyler had even ordered it with anchovies for me and helped clean up while we waited for delivery. I was going to have to do a little touching up with paint on the walls and ceiling, and suffice it to say I wouldn't be cooking anything in the immediate future, though Tyler thought the range could be saved to work another day.

Mom had phoned to let us know there was still no sign of Del, and Rooster had been in touch with Sheriff Wisniewski.

"The Sheriff said we could stop by the office tomorrow to file a report if he doesn't show up by then."

She went on to say Jack was driving her nuts with his bad behavior so I promised to pick him up in the morning and keep him with me for the day.

"Come for breakfast," Mom said.

"You won't be having boiled eggs, will you?"

"We can, dear, if you want them."

"No, no," I said hastily. "I prefer mine fried."

After we'd finished eating, Tyler was all business. He opened his laptop and pulled up a spreadsheet.

"Come and take a look. I want you to see where we are with your house."

Obediently I flopped onto the sofa, leaning into him, and peered at the screen.

"I went ahead and had a home inspection done. This is the report. You'll see there are no major problems. A few light fixtures need to be changed and some of the plumbing should be updated, otherwise this is really good and the house is solid."

I read through everything line by line even though some of it meant nothing to me. Ridge and fascia boards were not in my vocabulary, and muntins and mullions were a mystery. Still, if Tyler was happy then I was happy and I said so.

"It gets better," he said. "The inspector owes me a few favors so he did it for no charge."

"Yes!" I said and we high-fived.

"Moving on," Tyler switched to another screen. "We already talked about the house needing paint inside and out, and replacing the carpeting. Now, I know your thought was to have Rooster, Mike and Del do as much of the work as possible, but hear me out. The guys already have a lot on their plates at Welcome Home. Bringing them over here will take them away from that work, which I'm not sure you want to do. Also, who knows how long they'd need to get everything done?

"My suggestion is to bring in professionals. The painting can be done in two to three days and everything else in a day. We can have the property on the market by the weekend; maybe do an open house soon after."

"This is sounding expensive."

"Not really. Professionals have the equipment, tools and experience needed to do the best job. Do you know what it would cost to rent equipment for Rooster and the guys to use? Do any of them even have a clue how to lay carpet wall to wall?"

"Uh…" There was more to this than I'd realized.

"Besides, I've already negotiated discounts on your behalf. You're looking at a total bill of about $4,500. Maybe a bit more."

I choked. Concerned, Tyler went to the sink and poured a glass of water for me.

"I don't understand how spending nearly $5,000 – that I don't have, I might point out – is going to help me with this."

"It's going to bring you 10 to 15 thousand dollars more on the sale." Patiently Tyler explained. "Home buyers want move-in-ready properties. Most of them can't see potential or simply don't want to bother with fixing things up themselves. So they'll pay considerably more for something that's in perfect condition.

"As for paying the pros, I'll handle that for now. We can reconcile the costs when you sell. And with all honesty, if you had to buy paint, carpet and fixtures at retail, and rent tools, you'd probably still be looking at a $4,000 bill."

Yowser. I was really out of touch. When I'd bought my little house (where I actually live), Mom had given me several large throw rugs that she wasn't using to cover the old flooring, and I'd repainted bit by bit. Not that it took much, the place only had one bedroom and an open living and kitchen area.

"Sweetheart. Don't worry. It will all turn out for the best. I wouldn't steer you wrong."

Tyler's voice echoed his apprehension and I realized he must be taking my silence as a bad sign. With the back of my hand I gently stroked his cheek and smiled at him. "You," I paused for effect, "are amazing. If I had to deal with all this on my own I would make a complete mess of it."

"That would never happen. You're one of the most capable people I've ever known. And one of the sexiest." He pulled me to him. "Maybe the sexiest." Our lips met. Lucky me.

Eight

At seven the next morning I was tucking into fried eggs, bacon and cheesy grits at Mom's kitchen table. Life is good. I'd brought the dogs along for a ride and Angel and Vinny were now outside playing with Jack. They played rough and it was too much for Coco, so she stayed with me. Elaine just wasn't interested any more. I looked over at her as she lay on her bed, her head on the raised edge using it as a pillow, and thought how much I loved Rooster's sweet old pit bull.

A dog began barking, steadily and insistently. Coco stood up, cocking her head to the side, focused on the sound. Elaine cocked her ears and frowned.

"There's another dog somewhere." I looked questioningly at Mom who gave me a puzzled frown.

"We haven't taken in anyone new. Are you sure it isn't one of ours?"

"It's not."

The barking seemed to be coming closer. Coco and Elaine both stared at the door, my little toy poodle growling softly. The door opened and there stood a red-faced Mike. He had Polly with him, but this time she was on his shoulder and posturing proudly, chest puffed out … and barking.

"I can't get her to stop. Since we've had her she hasn't so much as squawked but she heard Vinny outside and suddenly found her voice."

Yikes. If she had to imitate one of the dogs, my yappy poodle was not a good choice. That high-pitched yelping could drive you nuts.

"Perhaps you could teach her to say a few words instead. Or sing a song. Preferably a lullaby."

"What? I can't hear you over the noise."

I dismissed the question with a wave and walked over to the coffee pot to pour myself a cup to go. Leaning against the counter I studied the macaw. She really was coming into her own. As annoying as the barking was, it was obvious the bird was having a good time and I was delighted to see her progress. As I passed Mike on my way to collect the dogs I yelled into his ear, "You're doing an amazing job with her." He smiled his gratitude and I made my escape.

I dropped Angel, Vinny and Coco at home. They'd sleep for the next few hours. Young Jack, on the other hand, still had energy but I'd have some time to stop at the park in between calls and run him through some basic commands.

The morning passed quickly enough and I figured I'd grab myself some lunch and enjoy it in the town square with Jack, who was finally slowing down. After I'd secured myself a reuben on focaccia bread I was lucky enough to find an empty bench facing the war memorial. It was a simple tower, etched with the names of Mallowapple residents who'd given their lives in service. Ours is a small town, so the list of names was not long. In fact, there was only one name for World War I but it was especially meaningful for me: Fireman First Class George Parrett, lost at sea 1918. He was my great great grandfather.

"Yo, Polly!"

Startled from my reveries on hearing my name I looked around and saw Dave Cartwright, an old school chum, waving. I raised my arm in return and he headed in my direction.

"Hey, Polly. How's it going? And Jack!" He got down on one knee and scratched the pup behind the ears, talking to him. "What are you doing with Polly?"

"I've got him for the day so … Wait a minute! How do you know Jack?"

"I never forget one of the dogs we save. Especially when they have as much personality as this one."

No way. Dave works at the County Animal Shelter. He must have confused my Jack with another dog, as improbable as that seemed, so I explained my history with the pup.

"Polly, I'm telling you, this dog was dropped off at the shelter by a family who said they couldn't handle him. It was the same old story of people getting the adorable little puppy only to find out it takes real work and commitment to care for him. He's a quality dog so I knew he wouldn't last long and, sure enough, he was adopted out in a couple of days."

"To Delbert Forlong?"

"Uhhh, Delbert sounds right, but I'm pretty sure his last name wasn't Forlong." Dave shrugged. "You know how it is, I remember the pets but I'm not so good with the people."

"I don't understand. How could a homeless man adopt a dog?"

"Homeless! What are you talking about? The guy had his own business. I remember distinctly because he was a private eye and I thought that was so cool."

Hoo, boy! Things just got really weird.

Nine

There was the usual exuberance from all the dogs as I pulled up at Welcome Home. From inside the house it sounded as if Polly Parrot was getting in on the action.

I yelled out as I walked through the front door, "I'm here!"

"As if we couldn't tell," my mother's disembodied voice replied.

I found her in the office with Rooster going over plans for the barn renovations.

"A group of volunteers from the VA is coming over this weekend to work," Mom explained. "We need to decide how to put them to use and what supplies we'll need. More truthfully, what supplies we can afford."

"Stop worrying about it. Tyler thinks we can expect a quick sale on Miss Ledbetter's house." Briefly, I filled them in on our conversation of the previous evening.

"Enough of that, though," Mom said. "What about Del?"

After my chat with Dave, I'd called Sheriff Wisniewski. He'd been unavailable so I'd left a detailed message, then called Mom to tell her what I'd found out.

"I never heard back from the Sheriff," I said.

"I talked to him." Rooster stood and twisted his torso back and forth to stretch it, commenting, "I can only sit so long before that low back pain starts."

I sympathized, but I wanted to hear what Wisniewski had to say.

"First, I went to the station this morning to report Del missing. I filled out the paperwork but Feliks," that's Sheriff Wisniewski, "said there wasn't much that could be done. No crime had been committed and the man didn't even have an official address."

It had been a rogue cop from Wisniewski's department who tried to frame Rooster for murder. You'd think that might have created tension but both men were better than that. In fact, as an active member of the VFW (Veterans of Foreign Wars), it was Wisniewski who had encouraged Rooster to join and they'd found a bond in service to their country.

"Anyway," Rooster went on, "Feliks called here late this afternoon. With the information from you, he found out that Del's real name is Fannin, not Forlong and he runs a detective agency out of Pittsfield. It's a one-man operation. He uses an answering service company to handle his calls."

"Pittsfield? Then what is he doing in Mallowapple masquerading as a homeless man?"

"He may be close to homeless. It seems he was probably living out of his office. He is state licensed however, which provided some other background details."

"Such as?"

"He actually was in the air force and there is an ex-wife and twin daughters."

"As they say, a good con stays close to the truth."

"But was this a con?" Mom sounded exasperated. "None of this makes sense. Why would anybody want to con themselves into a homeless shelter? This one in particular. We're pretty much broke all the time and we have no ties to anyone or anything of importance."

I shook my head, equally bewildered. "It certainly seems he was targeting Welcome Home or he wouldn't have needed a dog. Poor Jack. It does explain why he hadn't bonded with Del. And that part of Del's story was a total lie. That really ticks me off. He used the puppy and he was using us and I'm gonna make sure I tell him what I think about it."

"Calm down, dear. It doesn't help to get upset." Grr, I hate when my mother uses that placatory tone, even – no, especially – when she's right.

Still, I took a deep breath and managed to ask in a normal tone, "Was there anything else that Feliks could add to the equation?"

"If there was, he wasn't telling me," Rooster said, and the conversation petered out.

I offered to help Mom with dinner but I guess she could see I was still irritable, so she suggested Rooster give me his thoughts on sprucing up the furniture.

We walked in companionable silence to the barn, Rooster throwing wide the doors to allow the fading evening light in. Although the structure was fairly sound, tarpaulins had been laid over the pieces, "Just in case there's a roof leak or two," Rooster said. He caught hold of the corner of a tarp and peeled it back to reveal a solid wood dining set. "This is pecan wood." He rapped his knuckles on the top. "Those scuffs and scratches can all be buffed out and it will look like new. And there's two of these." He showed me a dresser with six curved drawers. "A little elbow grease and some new hardware and they'll be good to go."

With a flourish he tugged at the next cover. "And wait 'til you see this."

A dead body?

My mind couldn't quite wrap around the image of a man face-down and spread-eagled on the floor. Maybe it was because the back of his head was a mess of blood and bone. Rooster's military training kicked right in, though. He darted around me and knelt next to the body, placing his fingers on the neck where there should have been a steady pulse. Looking up, he shook his head.

"Call the police."

My cell phone was in my pocket. I knew I should reach in and dial 911, but my arm didn't seem to want to obey the commands my brain was sending. Instead, I began to shake uncontrollably. Realizing my distress, Rooster yanked the cover back over the man and, holding me firmly by the shoulders, led me outside where I sagged against the wall.

"Where's your phone?"

"Right pocket."

"Are you gonna be OK while I make the call?"

I nodded as he stepped away to talk. I caught snatches of his conversation, "...head wound...old barn...don't know..." and then, "Delbert Forlong."

In the fuzzy recesses of my mind it registered that the body was Del. In some keener part of my brain, however, my thought was, "What about Jack?"

As if he sensed he was on my mind, at that precise moment Jack came loping up, head high, proudly holding a big stick, which he promptly deposited at my feet and waited for me to throw.

"Oh, you poor puppy," I whispered and sank to the ground, taking him in my arms. That was when I noticed blood on the stick, and burst into tears.

Ten

Several hours later I sat at the kitchen table with Tyler holding my hand. Mallowapple is a small community and there's not much that escapes Tyler. As soon as he heard there was a problem at Welcome Home, he rushed out to do what he could to help. I'd spent nearly an hour being interviewed by the police. Sheriff Wisniewski was leading the investigation.

Unsettled by the activity, all the dogs were sticking close to us while Mom made another pot of hot tea. I'd had more than enough already and really needed to go to the bathroom but I wasn't ready yet to relinquish my hold on Tyler.

"I don't know why I'm such a wreck. It's not like this is the first murder I've been involved with."

"It's the first where you've known the victim," Tyler put things in perspective as the Sheriff walked into the room, Rooster at his side.

"The body has been taken away and my men are now sealing the crime scene. Polly, I'll need you at the station as soon as you feel up to it, to read over and sign your witness statement. Meanwhile, if any of you think of anything else, even if it seems trivial, call immediately."

"Do you have any suspects?" Tyler looked worried. "A man has been murdered practically on the doorstep and the killer is still out there."

"Are we safe?" I was particularly concerned for Mom. "Can you leave someone here to keep an eye on things?"

"I don't have the manpower for that. You do need to be very vigilant, though. Keep doors and windows locked, even during the day, and don't go out alone."

"That's not very encouraging." My tone was sour. "Do you at least know if this was a random murder or was Del targeted?"

"I hope to know more tomorrow." With that, Wisniewski turned and left.

"Well that wasn't exactly helpful. For all we know there's a crazed killer on the loose just waiting to take pot shots at us."

Rooster squeezed my shoulder. "Give the man a break, Polly. If he thought we were really in danger he'd figure something out. And I'll keep watch tonight. After this, I'm not sure I could sleep anyway."

"Rooster, I hope you're not staying up for my sake. I can take care of myself," Mom said. "I've ridden 1200 pound horses over five-foot-high fences, given birth to three babies, even hiked the Appalachian Trail. I have a gun and I know how to use it. Don't let these wheels fool you." She patted the wheels on her chair.

"Edwina, I know you're one tough lady," Always the diplomat, that Rooster, "but for my own piece of mind I want to be sure no-one messes up all the good work we've done around here."

"Maybe none of us needs to worry." Tyler reached for his phone. "I have an idea." He walked away from us as he appeared to peruse his contacts then turned, leaning against the counter and holding the phone to his ear.

"Hi, K9 Security, Tyler Breslin here. I know it's getting late but we have something of a crisis at Welcome Home and could really use your services. Call me, please, as soon as you get this message." He left his contact details then hung up, nodding at us with a satisfactory air. "We'll have the professionals take care of safety. And before any of you object because of the cost, it's on me. Consider it a donation to the cause."

Within a couple of hours Jake from K9 Security was at the farm with Moe at his side. We all listened carefully as he talked. "We'll set up a nightly schedule for you with a handler and a dog. It's a small area to patrol so I don't think you need more than that. For tonight, I'll be here, but we have half a dozen other guys we might rotate through.

"First thing I want to do is scope out the area with one of you so Moe and I get familiar with the lay of the land. It's important that when we're on patrol you don't come outside without alerting us first. All our guys carry handguns and the dogs are pretty much lethal weapons so…no surprises, OK?"

Moe didn't exactly look lethal at the moment as he lazily scratched his nose with a paw. Jake noticed the direction of my gaze. "I haven't given him the work command yet."

I put my hands up in a defensive gesture. "No need to explain. I've seen one of your dogs in action, remember, and it was awesome. I'm just really grateful that you're able to help us out."

"I second that," Mom said. "Now, tell me what I can get for you? Coffee? Treats for the dog?"

"No ma'am…"

"Edwina," Mom interjected.

Jake smiled. "That's nice of you, Edwina, but we have everything we need, and the dogs are not allowed treats when on duty. That's something they get from their handlers for a job well done."

"OK, then," Rooster stepped forward. "How about Mike and I show you around?"

The three of them moved off, leaving me with Tyler and Mom.

"Are you going to stay here tonight, Polly?"

"I can't, Mom. I've got to get home to take care of the cats." Amber, Taz and Ditto could be pretty self-sufficient if need be, but I really didn't like leaving them alone for too long.

Mom and Tyler exchanged a look. I knew that look. They thought I was being rash. Before either of them could say a word, though, I made my feelings known.

"There's nothing to suggest I could be in any danger. Everything points to Welcome Home or something personal in Del's life. Besides, I have an attack cat."

The dogs could only be relied upon to kiss someone to pieces but Ditto, my tuxedo cat, was very territorial and could be meaner than a junkyard dog if he felt threatened.

"That is true," Tyler conceded. "But I'm following you home so I can check out the house before I leave you there alone."

Of course you are, my knight in shining armor.

Eleven

Polly the parrot had really come into her own, and as she shed her fear so Mike began to shed his shyness. To distract her from the annoying barking, he'd decided to teach her to talk. Already she was saying "hello" and "pretty girl." Right now she was entertaining the volunteers from the VA who'd come out to help work on the barn conversion. There were also a few who'd responded to our email plea after signing up at the jamboree a few weeks ago. All in all we had about fifteen helpers, which was fabulous.

We were taking a break for lunch. Long ago my dad had built a big old brick grill outside; now Tyler's dad was wielding tongs over hot dogs and sweet sausages that he was dishing out to the helpers. Foil-wrapped potatoes were cooking in the hot coals and Mom had made up a huge batch of her homemade coleslaw along with one of my favorites, oatmeal apple crisp. We may not be able to pay people for the work but we could sure feed them.

"Hey, Polly! Give me a kiss!" How rude.

I looked around to see who was being so forward before it dawned on me the words were not meant for me. Polly Parrot's admirers were throwing kisses at her. In turn she was making kissing sounds back while lifting one leg and waving it. I couldn't deny, she was darn cute.

Mike had her on his shoulder. He must be clipping her wings so she couldn't fly away. I really should chat with him about her care and condition. I was feeling a bit guilty for leaving him to take charge of her. After all, Naomi Ledbetter did specify me as her care-giver.

Noticing me watching, Mike lifted his chin in salutation and headed my way. The day, as well as the work, was quite warm so this was the first time I'd seen him wearing shorts. Because of the artificial limb his gait was just slightly off, but I marveled at the technology and his ability to use it.

"You know," I said as he neared, "with long pants on I doubt anyone would know you had a prosthetic leg."

"Yep. Things aren't always what they seem."

"Not what it seems. Not what it seems," chanted his feathered friend.

"Gracious." I was astonished. "Did she just pick that up?"

Mike shook his head. "I can't take credit for her verbal skills. I think Mrs. Ledbetter must have taught her quite a vocabulary. That's the first time I've heard her say that."

"She's becoming a real chatty Kathy, then. Or, I should say Polly."

Mike chuckled and immediately Polly mimicked him. He reached up to scratch her neck and as he did so I noticed an unusual tattoo on his arm, partly hidden by the sleeve of his t-shirt. It looked like some sort of bird with bared teeth.

70

"What's the meaning of the tat?"

His face turned hard. "Nothing."

"Sorry. I didn't mean to upset you. It's just unusual and …"

"I said it's nothing!"

His words were like a verbal slap. I took an involuntary step back and, of course, stepped in one of the holes the dogs had industrially been digging. My already bum knee gave out on me and I crashed down onto my hip.

"Ow!" I sucked air through my teeth as a stinging pain embraced my rear. Mike's mood did another one-eighty as he crouched beside me, evoking nothing but concern.

"Are you OK?" Obviously not. I bit back the words, though, not wanting to trigger "Menacing Mike's" return, and accepted his assistance getting back on my feet. Well, foot actually. I could only put my weight on one leg – again.

You're probably thinking I'm a real klutz. Honestly, I don't know why this stuff keeps happening to me. As a kid I was in Miss Rispin's ballet class for a long time so I'm well-trained in balance and… Oh! Come to think of it, Mom pulled me from the classes when Miss Rispin suggested I might be more suited to clogging.

Mike helped me to the picnic bench where my half-eaten sandwich waited for me. It had become a little chewy but I was hungry so I gnawed on it while wondering what the heck was wrong with the young veteran. There wasn't much time to ponder the question, however. Rooster, who was in charge of operations, called the helpers to order and everyone returned to their duties of sanding, scraping, painting, hammering and whatever else was needed.

Doing my best to ignore my discomfort, I rose to the occasion and, by the end of the day, we had ourselves a pretty nice bunkhouse with six areas blocked out for individual rooms. They weren't actual rooms because the walls didn't go all the way to the roof, but at least they would give the residents some privacy.

It was thrilling to see such improvement and the mood amongst the workers was downright elated, with plenty of back-slapping and high-fiving as they said their good-byes and headed home. For a while, I even forgot about the murder.

An arm came across my shoulder, giving me a squeeze. "I think we deserve a major pat on the back."

"More than that," I said, hugging Tyler's sister, Suzette. "I see a big glass of wine in my future. Care to join me?"

"You're on!"

Suzette is a couple of years younger than Tyler. She's beautiful to look at and has a beautiful personality to go with it and I thought the world of her. She tucked her arm in mine and together we strolled to the house. Well, I sort of stumbled. The dogs all fell in behind us as if we were a pair of pied pipers, including Frank, Tyler's big, goofy bloodhound mix.

"Where were you all day?" I asked. "I hardly saw you."

"Working with Mike cutting wood for framing and sub-flooring."

"Don't you find him a little unsettling?"

"In what way?"

"Let's get our wine and find a quiet place to talk."

So we did, and while we sipped I told Suzette about Mike's reaction when I mentioned the tattoo, and his reluctance to talk about his family.

"Have you talked to Rooster about this?"

"Sure. He says to give Mike more time, but his mood swings really worry me. We know he has PTSD and it scares me that he could have an episode and harm Mom in some way. In fact," I leaned in close and dropped my voice to a whisper, "I can't help but wonder if he had anything to do with Del's death."

"Polly, that's a shocking thing to say. Do you have any evidence?"

"No, and I feel guilty for saying it. But you hear stories of people who have been hurt by someone with post-traumatic stress syndrome. There was that young war veteran not long ago who beat his girlfriend to death. He said she just set him off but he doesn't remember how."

"You're over-thinking this, Polly. I've seen no evidence of anything but a gentle soul. As I recall, drugs and alcohol were involved in the incident you're talking about and Mike doesn't drink or have access to drugs, at least as far as I know. Seriously, Welcome Home is all about helping people like Mike. Let's find a way to do that before we condemn him."

She was right, of course. I was just about to say that when I glanced up and realized Mike was watching us. We'd settled ourselves on the back patio. Mike's room was on the second floor above us. His window was closed, but I had no idea if he could have heard our conversation. Weakly, I waved a hand at him. He didn't move and his face remained completely impassive. Rats.

Twelve

It had happened again. Someone had disappeared from the farmhouse. This time, it was Mike. Polly, the macaw, was gone, too.

A mid-morning call from Mom alerted me while I was walking Chester, a Newfoundland Rottweiler mix who was one of my new clients from the pet-sitters' jamboree. Technically, Chester was still a puppy – a 130 pound puppy. He may have seemed as big as a grizzly bear but he had the heart of a teddy bear. For nearly an hour he'd been romping round with a high-energy fox terrier who went by the not unlikely name of Pistol.

I'd planned to use the afternoon to spy on my crew. That sounds terrible, I know. Here's the thing, though, my first obligation is to my clients and their pets. To ensure my staff are fulfilling that obligation I make it a point to check on them unexpectedly from time to time. The crew I have now is pretty great, but you can never be too careful. I once called a walker and asked where she was. Blithely she announced she was walking her charges as scheduled. That was a lie. I'd been sitting in my car down the street, had seen her arrive at the client's house and not leave. She was pretty red-faced when I knocked on the door. She was also without a job.

Anyway, the point I was meaning to make is that I was able to free up the rest of my day to help look for Mike.

I just had to get Chester home. Wouldn't you know, however, that wasn't going to be so easy?

Chester was tired and ready for a nap. Problem was, he was ready for his nap now! He flopped down, closed his eyes and was asleep in an instant. I nudged him, shook him, called his name and he unconsciously rolled onto his back exposing his belly for a rub.

I bobbed around acting excited and shouting in a high-pitched voice, "Walkies! Treats! Cats! Good boy! Come on!" None of it had any effect, but the dog park contingent were highly amused. Unfortunately, they consisted of two elderly ladies and a wizened old man. At this time of day during the week all the young muscle was at work.

Crouching down I tested the feasibility of carrying Chester to the car. Holy smokes! Even without my knee and hip problems, there was no way. I was going to have to call in the cavalry.

You're thinking I'm referring to Tyler, aren't you? Wrong! I scrolled through my contacts list and found K9 Security. "Um, Jake? Do you think I could hire you for just half an hour or so?"

"Polly, don't ever change," Mat Abaroa said. "Who else would give us so much to smile about?" He and Jake had both come to my rescue and between them, lifting Chester had been a breeze. The dog park oldsters had cheered as they carried him to my car, still firmly in the land of slumber. The guys had then followed me to

Chester's home and reversed the procedure, depositing the pup on his bed in the laundry room, which was his pseudo crate. I tucked his favorite toy between his front paws, made sure the door was closed and locked up the house, meeting Mat and Jake outside.

Putting on a business air to hide my embarrassment I asked how much I owed for their services.

"We don't want anything. We had the time to spare and it's always fun when we see you." Did I detect a hint of sarcasm there? I decided to ignore it.

"I can't tell you how much I appreciate this. I really need to get to the farmhouse – Mike has gone missing."

Of course, then I had to tell them what happened.

"Who did we have on patrol there last night?" Mat asked of his partner.

"It was Samson, with Delilah." For real?

Both men looked concerned.

"They're a good team," Jake assured me while Mat stepped away from us, his phone to his ear, dialing Samson.

"I don't doubt it."

Mat was pacing as he talked. Snatches of words floated our way but they were no more than dust in the wind. After a few moments he strode back to us.

"Samson is adamant no-one left the house before his shift ended at seven. He says Rooster came out with coffee just before he and Delilah headed home, and that's it." Looking back and forth between Jake and me he added, "I think we should consider extending the patrols."

Mat's words made feel a bit panicky. When Del disappeared he ended up dead, and I was beginning to have visions of Mike with a bloody head and Polly Parrot stiff and cold beside him.

"Let's not panic," I said, pretending to be cool-headed and reasonable. "Before anything is decided I need to speak with Mom and Tyler. Besides, Mike could have left of his own accord. The word is out he's missing and, let's face it, how hard should it be to find a one-legged man with a parrot on his shoulder?"

Mat bit his lip and looked at Jake who dead-panned, "Aargh, we be lookin' fer Long John Silver." At which they both burst into laughter.

"This is hardly a laughing matter!"

"Don't you realize what you just said? A one-legged man with a parrot on his shoulder. It sounds like a pirate."

"Oh, my." Indeed it did, and I recognized the silliness and joined in the laughter and felt much better for it.

A little later, hysteria aside, we became serious again.

"Honestly, I'm just so confused right now. The most important thing is finding Mike, but I'm also responsible for the bird. Then there's a murder to solve, a killer is still on the loose, I'm worried about Mom and I need to figure out what to do with Jack."

"Anything we can do to help, anything at all, just name it," Jake said.

"Have I told you how glad I am to have met you two?"

"Aw shucks," Mat quipped. So I slapped him on the arm. It was like hitting steel tubing; my hand stung and my fingers wouldn't bend. So when my phone rang an instant later I had to contort my body to try and reach into my right jeans pocket with my left arm. Mat offered to help but I figured it was time I showed I could be independent. It wasn't easy but I managed to retrieve the device. By then it had stopped ringing and gone to voicemail but I saw that it was Mom and hit redial.

"Thank goodness," was Mom's urgent greeting. "There's been a sighting on the Old South Road. Mamie Soames called the sheriff's office and said she'd seen an alien creature walking there. Ruby Peach took the call and was going to hang up when Mamie said something about the alien giving birth to a multicolored babe. That got Ruby's attention and she got from Mamie that the alien was carrying something brightly colored in its arms. She figured it might be the parrot and called here."

"How did Ruby know about Mike and Polly being missing?"

"I called the hair salon."

That explained it. Drop a word at Combing Attractions Salon and it would become a tsunami in no time at all. The whole of Mallowapple would know about Mike by now.

"Right. I'll get going and see if I can spot them."

"Should you be doing this alone?"

"I think I'm covered," I said, smiling at Mat and Jake.

Thirteen

The K9 Security duo were more than willing to provide backup for me but one of them needed to get back to their own business. So it was decided Mat would ride along and I'd drop him off later, which gave me an opportunity to tell him about Mamie Soames.

"No-one knows just how old she is, including Mamie. She's as nutty as a fruitcake and pretty much blind as a bat. In her whole life she'd never been to the movies, so several decades ago she upped and decided to go. The movie happened to be Alien, and it changed Mamie's life. Since then, she sees people birthing bioforms about once a month."

Mat gave me one of those "you've got to be kidding" looks.

"Honestly. It's a real problem when kids knock on her door at Halloween holding baskets of candy in front of them."

We were on the Old South Road now and Mat was silent. I wasn't sure if it was because he was concentrating on looking for Mike or if he just didn't know what to say after the Mamie revelation.

The road was pretty typical for this part of Maine; narrow and winding, uninhabited for miles at a time and flanked by pines with a few broadleaf trees mixed in. If you followed it long enough you'd eventually get to a major highway that would take you all the way south to Florida. Mamie would have been driving it because she was going to pick up a bottle of Pop Stegall's herbal remedy, which was really corn liquor flavored with wild horseradish. Whatever. It seemed to be working for her.

We'd passed the turn-off to Pop's property now and I slowed down so we could eyeball through the tree line in case Mike was trying to hide from traffic. Somehow I didn't think he'd try and flag down any passing vehicles.

Mat pulled the sunglasses from his face and pressed his head against the side window.

"See something?"

He grunted and sat back again. "I guess not." Then he shook his head. "It doesn't make sense that Mike would just up and leave like this. What could possibly have caused him to run off?"

"Uh, dunno." Except he might have heard me suggest he was a potential murderer.

We lapsed into silence, me dwelling on my guilt for being suspicious of Mike and worrying what might become of him and Polly.

"There!" Mat's shout jerked me from my absorption. "Straight ahead; it looks like someone on the side of the road."

Sure enough, as we drew closer, the vague shape morphed into a human being. A little closer still and we saw it was Mike, sitting cross-legged on the berm. I say cross-legged but that wasn't strictly true as his prosthetic leg was bent at a crazy angle.

I pulled off the road and parked. Mike didn't even look our way; his whole posture was of defeat. Mat reached for the door handle but I tugged on his arm. "Let me do this." He must have seen the determination in my expression so gave a brief nod and let me go.

As I closed the van door I realized I was trembling, and it occurred to me the demon I was about to face was the fear of rejection by this young man who I'd rejected when he needed all the friends he could get. And where was Polly? Please, Lord, don't let something have happened to her.

"Hello, hello!"

I laughed in relief. There she was tucked inside Mike's shirt.

"Polly, you beautiful girl. I am so happy to see you." I softened my voice. "And Mike, I'm even happier to see you."

Finally, he looked at me. His face wore a mask of pain and betrayal.

"Can I sit down?... Please?"

He gave a slight lift of his shoulders, so I eased myself onto the ground in front of him.

"Mike, I've been a complete ass. It's not the first time but it's certainly one of the worst. I should never have talked behind your back; I should have come to you to talk about my concerns. Please give me a chance to make it up to you."

He began chewing on his lower lip, obviously unsure what to say or do.

"I'm so sorry, Mike. Please tell me what I can do to make things better?"

"Give me a kiss, give me a kiss." Polly Parrot spoke with impeccable timing.

This time, it was Mike who began to laugh, then I joined in and we just couldn't seem to stop until Mat stood beside us. "What on earth is going on?"

Fourteen

There'd been a lot of back-slapping and hugging at Welcome Home when we returned with Mike. Turned out he had nearly been hit by an eighteen-wheeler hurtling round a bend. The driver probably never saw him, but he'd leapt away and fallen into a stony ditch that ran alongside the road, breaking his prosthetic leg and smashing his hip. He managed to drag himself back up to the road, hoping to thumb a lift somewhere because he certainly couldn't walk. The thing that really tore him up, though, was that Polly, who was secured in his shirt, could have been crushed when he fell.

Once again, I was more than a little thankful for Mat's presence. He got Mike into the van and we drove straight to the hospital to get him checked out. While Mat waited with him I took the parrot to Doctor Jim, our local vet, who gave her a thorough going over before pronouncing her a little stressed, but otherwise fine.

Mike had X-rays taken, which showed a lot of bruising and the need for a chiropractor. Thankfully, nothing was broken and he was released with pain killers and instructions to alternate ice and heat and be careful. He and Polly had now been reunited and sent to rest, while Rooster worked on the damaged prosthetic.

"Think you can fix it?"

Rooster peered at me over the top of his glasses. "Nothing actually broke. These things are made really strong; the material didn't even bend, it just went out of alignment. All I have to do is undo a couple parts, realign it and put it back together. Mike could easily do it himself if he had a few tools with him. I'm gonna put together a small pack he can carry in a pocket, in case anything happens again."

"Maybe you shouldn't give it to him 'til we're sure he's going to stay."

"That's not really our call to make, is it?"

"Then I'm going to do everything I can to persuade him this is the best place to be."

"Atta girl," Rooster grinned.

Fifteen

Suzette and I were tucking into grilled bacon and pimento cheese sandwiches with crunchy fries. We were lunching at Bennie's Diner, Mallowapple's favorite eating place and gossip hub. When she wasn't helping at the halfway house, Suzette worked in her family's real estate firm, and we tried to get together for lunch every couple of weeks or so.

Today we were discussing the murder of Del Forlong, or Fannin, I should call him.

"And Rooster hasn't been able to get anything out of the Sheriff?"

I shook my head. "If Wisniewski has any idea why Del was posing as a homeless vet he's not telling anyone, not even Rooster, which makes me think he just doesn't know."

"Do you girls need more coffee?" Nita, the diner's owner and gossip-in-chief hovered beside us.

"Not me," I said, while Suzette shook her head. Nita promptly put the pot on the table and settled herself into an empty chair.

"I heard you mention the murder. What's the latest?" Elbows on the table and chin on her clasped hands, Nita leaned towards us.

"There's nothing," I said.

"Oh, come on. I know Sheriff Wisniewski talks to Rooster. You must know something."

"Really," I shrugged, "we haven't heard a thing."

Nita sat back with a grunt. "Unless I come up with something soon people will begin to think I'm losing my edge to Combing Attractions."

There was a bit of an ongoing feud between the diner and the hair salon as to who got the best gossip. It could be really annoying at times, but right now an idea was forming in my mind.

"Nita, how about we start a rumor and catch a killer?"

Suzette raised her eyebrows at me. "Is this something I might regret being a part of?" But Nita was instantly hooked.

"Tell me what you want?"

Sixteen

Being a pet-sitter is not always easy, but then there are times it's just plain fun.

Tina was spending a week with a bulldog by the name of Otis, while his pet parents romped around Cozumel. It happened that it was Otis's birthday today, and we'd been asked to give him a "pawty" and video the happy event. The preparation had all been done by Tina; my job was to run the video and take pictures.

Otis was already in his pawty hat when I got there. As I used my phone to film, Tina brought out a pupcake she'd made using a recipe from a book called The BARKtender's Guide. She'd shaped it and decorated it with peanut butter frosting to look like a dog's face. In it were three lit candles and she sang Happy Birthday as she presented the pupcake to Otis, whipping the candles out before he devoured them with his cake. The Pawty Animal Pupcake, made with oatmeal and watermelon, was a huge hit and Tina confided there were a couple more for Otis to enjoy another day.

When it came to opening presents, no dog could have been more excited. Otis snorted and whuffled as he ripped the paper off the hide-a-squirrel from his parents – a soft tree trunk with holes in which plush squirrel toys were hidden. He poked his head in the holes as Tina played peek-a-boo with the squirrels, and carried them off proudly when she let him have one.

From Pets are People, Too he received an organic elk antler that he promptly began to chew and drool over. All in all, it was a great success and I left soon after, giving Otis a generous scratch on the rump.

Tyler's car was in my driveway as I pulled in. It wasn't like him to turn up unannounced, so my first feelings of pleasure turned to concern that something was wrong.

The dogs gave me their usual ecstatic greeting as I went in the house, but Tyler stood with his arms crossed and his expression stern. Uh oh.

"I hear something's been found at the farmhouse."

"Hi, honey." I tried to sound normal but my voice came out as a squeak. How had he heard so soon? Surely Suzette didn't rat me out?

In answer to my unasked questions he continued. "I stopped into the diner for lunch right after you and Suzette left." Yep, that would do it. "Nita told me it was something valuable. In fact, she told everybody in the place that an item of great value had been discovered out at Welcome Home and you have it in your possession. Of course, I tried to call you," Oh, yeah, I'd turned my ringer off while I was filming Otis, "but you didn't answer. So I called Suzette."

Not even Tyler's sister could resist him when he was determined to get the truth. She would have caved and told him everything. I didn't blame her; I would have done the same.

I swallowed and took a deep breath. "Nothing was happening about finding Del's killer or why he was pretending to be someone he wasn't. So I..."

"So you what? So you invented a story that would put you right in the killer's crosshairs. What kind of lame-brained idea was that? And how do you know nothing's happening? Did it never occur to you that this is a police investigation and there's no reason they would include you in it? Maybe Sheriff Wisniewski deliberately kept you in the dark because he knows you just can't stop meddling where you don't belong."

By now my face was burning and my emotions had run the gamut from shock to hurt, to anger. "It's not meddling; I was trying to help." Damn, I was going to cry.

"How the heck is it helping when you put yourself in danger? And maybe others, too?" Tyler wasn't backing down. Worst thing was, I was beginning to realize he was right, but I couldn't bring myself to admit it. Instead, I stamped my foot – jeez, how juvenile was that? – and yelled back.

"Someone had to make a move. You just don't have the guts to do it."

As soon as the words were out of my mouth, I regretted them. Tyler's eyes went wide then his lips tightened. He gave a curt nod and strode past me, and out the door. I heard his car start up followed by a piercing wail, which happened to be me. My chest felt tight and it was hard to breath. I sank to my knees, dropped my head back and moaned Heavenward. How could I have been so stupid? How could I have said something so mean?

Upset, the dogs crowded round me, whining, and I buried my face in their necks, sobbing loudly. Had I just destroyed the best thing in my life?

I didn't hear the door open, but strong arms came around me, drawing me close. A hand pulled my head into a shoulder, and over and over a voice said, "I'm sorry, I'm sorry," as I was rocked gently. Tyler. He'd come back.

"Yum buk," I mumbled into his collar.
"What?" He released his hold on my head and stroked the hair away from my face.

I sniffed and took a steadying breath. "You came back."

"How can I leave when I'm so in love with you?" Wow. There aren't many things that can shut me up, but that was one of them. He kissed me softly on the lips and of course I burst into tears all over again.

Seventeen

At Tyler's insistence I'd had to come clean with Mom and Rooster about starting the rumor. Concerned for my safety they'd insisted I come and stay at the farmhouse where there were lots of people to keep an eye on me. Meekly I'd agreed, knowing it would make Tyler happy.

Business was running smoothly right now and I'd put Tina in charge for a couple of days, thinking this might be a good opportunity to go through the furniture and furnishings from my inheritance. So Rooster and I were doing inventory to decide which things to keep and which to donate or dump.

"Most of the soft furnishings aren't worth keeping." Rooster gestured to the ugly yellow sofa, "but these," he placed his hands on a pair of wing back chairs, "will clean up real good."

Rooster read the doubt on my face as I looked at the pukey-mustard chairs.

"You buy these new today, you'd probably be looking at upwards of $2,000 each."

My mouth dropped. "Then how come we couldn't sell them?"

"I guess most folk don't look beyond the dirty fabric, but they don't even need new padding. In fact, they don't look like they were ever sat in much. If we can pick up some cheap upholstery fabric I can have them good as new. It just takes a little time and patience."

"Who's going to do all the sewing?"

"There's not much to do, most of it's stapling. Besides, your mom's pretty handy with the sewing machine."

OK, who was I to disagree?

"What else do you think we can use?"

"Pretty much all the wood furniture. I showed you some pieces when we, er, found, er..."

Rooster's voice trailed off as we both remembered finding Del's body. There was an awkward moment of silence, broken when Mike walked in with Polly the parrot on his arm. "I wondered if I could help at all," he said.

"Help, help," the bird shrieked, dancing a jig and bobbing up and down, causing us all to laugh.

"Yeah, Mike," Rooster waved him over. "Help me move some of these boxes out of the way so we can get a look at the furniture behind."

Mike stepped forward, then stopped uncertainly. "Polly," he looked at me, "would you hold Polly for a while?"

I sighed. This name thing was really irritating me, but I smiled and held out my arm, "Come here, pretty girl."

Mike dug his hand into a pocket and pulled out some nuts for me to use as encouragement and Polly stepped onto my arm. I kept her occupied while the guys cleared the way, then we all eyed a dark-stained credenza.

It looked pretty out of place among Naomi Ledbetter's rather ornate things; this was square-cornered and plain.

"Isn't that art-deco style?" I asked.

"It's the kind of thing that was popular in the 1950s," Rooster said. "Does seem out of place with everything else, I agree." He ran his hands over the wood. "Teak, I think."

"Aunty pan, aunty pan," Polly said. At least, that's what it sounded like.

I raised my eyes at Mike and he held out his hands in a "who knows" gesture.

"Oh well, let's look at some other stuff," I said, but Polly had something else in mind. She hopped from my arm onto the credenza, yelling her aunty pan thing followed by "Don't tell," over and over.

Mike reached for her, making soothing sounds, but she avoided him while keeping up the chatter and then began pecking at the back of the credenza. It was made of that cheap fiber board, and her powerful beak was more than a match for it; a macaw's bite is as strong as a large dog.

"Hey!" Mike tapped her on the head to get her attention. She stopped ripping at the board, puffed out her chest and gave one last, "Aunty pan. Don't tell," before going back to her perch on Mike's arm.

"What was that all about?" I shook my head.

"It sounded to me like she was saying panel, not pan," Mike said.

"Aunty panel? That still doesn't make sense."

"Well, she's a bird," Mike gave a look that said, "duh."

"You're right. Why should I expect her to make sense? She's just making noise."

"Maybe not." Rooster was bending over the back of the credenza, Swiss army knife in hand. He straightened his back. "I think she might have been saying, 'Antique panel.' "

I gave him a questioning look and he held up a finger, indicating I should wait. He turned to Mike, "Son, help me turn this thing around.

"See here." Rooster pulled back more of the board where Polly had loosened it. "There's a piece of carved wood underneath, and it looks real old to me."

Together, Rooster and Mike carefully peeled away the fiber board and we were presented with a panel, made up of sections decorated with an intricate pattern of stars. At any rate, to me they looked like stars; Rooster and Mike started talking about polygons and geometric rays. Huh? So I interrupted.

"Basically, you're saying this is an antique panel?"

"Antique panel. Don't tell," Polly squawked, looking pleased with herself.

"I'm saying," Rooster spoke slowly, "we might have found the reason Del was in here."

Eighteen

Paul Schroeder looked more like an aging hippie than an antiques dealer; a tie-dye bandana holding down long hair, and a droopy mustache framing his mouth. He'd pulled up in a new Mercedes though. I wasn't quite sure how that fit with the whole "free spirit" thing but the guy was donating his time and expertise, so I wasn't going to question it.

After finding the panel yesterday we decided the smart thing would be to get it looked at by an expert. Of course, we didn't know any, but the VFW came through again when Rooster put out a call for help. Schroeder was a member in Greenville, but he'd driven over to Mallowapple to help us out.

"Well, what's the verdict?" Sheriff Wisniewski was getting impatient. We'd contacted him as soon as we figured we might have found something of relevance to Del's murder. He'd been pacing up and down for the last fifteen minutes, but Schroeder wasn't going to be rushed.

Actually, most of the Welcome Home family had crowded in to the barn and there was an air of excitement between us. Even Mom had wheeled herself over and Tyler had brought Suzette to join in the spectacle. I suspected Schroeder was enjoying the notoriety and he had spent a lot of time on his knees inspecting the panel while emitting a steady stream of "ahs" and "hmms." When he finally tried to stand his knee gave out on him, and he was about to clutch the credenza when Tyler grabbed him and helped him up.

Clearing his throat, he gazed slowly around at his audience then directed his attention to Wisniewski. "The verdict, Sheriff, is that you have a late fifteenth or early sixteenth century Spanish or Moroccan door panel. This particular style of paneling originated in Maghribi, North Africa and spread to Spain in the fourteenth century. There's a strikingly similar panel in the Museo de la Alhambra and a comparable pair of doors in the David collection in Denmark."

Schroeder sucked in a deep breath but I figured I'd better butt in before he continued his Antiques Road Show parody.

"That's all very interesting. I think we all want to know the same thing, though. What's it worth?"

Schroeder looked a little miffed at being cut off mid-monologue. "It's impossible to say for sure without more detailed examination, and carbon dating to confirm the age."

"Then you're not sure it is genuine?" Mom sounded disappointed.

"I am sure," Schroeder was emphatic, "but the rest of the world requires proof. I expect you understand that Sheriff, more than most."

In the background someone said, "We still don't know if it's valuable."

"Just give us your best estimate." The Sheriff fixed an unwavering stare on the antiques dealer.

"Keeping in mind that it does have some small nail holes where it's been attached to the credenza, and I haven't been able to examine it closely..."

Wisniewski made a low growling noise and Schroeder gave him a nervous glance. "Uh, yes. Well, I can tell you a similar panel sold at auction a few years ago for $75,000."

There was a collective gasp. I clutched at Tyler's arm and we exchanged shocked looks. "You're saying this thing is worth that much money?" My voice was actually quavering.

"Perhaps more, or you might get less. Selling at auction is very volatile. I should think you'd certainly get $50,000 though."

Nineteen

Everyone was on tenterhooks. At one and the same time I think we were all elated over our found treasure, and really nervous we were no closer to finding the killer.

Schroeder was making arrangements for the credenza to be picked up the next day and taken to a secure place for examination. Meanwhile, it had been brought into the house where Rooster and Tyler planned to watch over it through the night. K9 Securities were doubling their guard outside and the rest of us were hoping to get some sleep.

Polly the parrot had been showing off all evening by talking up a storm. No-one complained, though. After all, she was the one who'd directed our attention to the door panel.

"Old Miss Ledbetter must have taught her to say 'Antique panel. Don't tell,' and shown her where the panel was hidden," Mike said.

"Oh, come on," I rolled my eyes, "I doubt she could associate the credenza with a few words she learned to mimic."

Mike looked offended as he handed Polly one of her favorite pine nut treats. "Birds are a lot smarter than people think, and macaws are among the most intelligent."

"I'll take your word for it. And no matter what, she's the greatest bird in the world as far as I'm concerned. I would have dumped that credenza with hardly a second look."

Mike's expression softened as I scratched the bird's head. We were the last two in the kitchen, finishing up the dishes before heading to bed. It felt good that Mike and I could chat like old friends; the tension of a few days ago now behind us.

"How about a hot chocolate to take with you?"

Mike nodded his appreciation and sat at the table as I put water in the kettle and grabbed the chocolate from the cupboard before plopping down opposite him to wait for the water to boil. He was wearing a short-sleeved t-shirt that exposed the bird tattoo on his arm. I couldn't help but look at it for a moment, then quickly glanced away. Mike caught the look, however, and I bit my lips, feeling awkward.

"Sorry, I'm not prying. You don't have to tell me anything."

He dropped his head and began to drum his fingers on the table and I thought I'd just messed up again. Then he surprised me when he began to speak.

"I always loved birds, even when I was really young, but my family was so poor they couldn't even afford a bird as a pet. There was a bird store in the town; it started as a place for people to buy bird feed and cages and such. Then customers began asking the owner if he would watch their pets when they went away, and so he started a boarding business alongside his store.

"Mr. Votaw was his name, but everyone called him Mr. V. He had a gray parrot of his own, Biggles, that hung out in the shop with him. I'd go in just to see Biggles and Mr. V. He was really a good man, started to let me help out with the birds he was looking after. He'd give me a quarter here and there; I thought I was rich."

The kettle whistled and I jumped up to fix the hot chocolate. Mike went silent 'til I set a mug in front of him.

"One day, a guy came into the store while I was there. He had this tattoo on his arm and I just couldn't get my eyes off it. He saw me watching and came to talk with me. I thought he was being nice but Mr. V. later told me to stay away from him, that he was bad news.

"A few days later I came across the guy again. He recognized me, told me he had racing pigeons and did I want to see them? Of course, I didn't give a thought to Mr. V.'s words of warning and off I went. That was the beginning."

Mike wrapped his hands around his mug and sipped at the drink; I kept quiet, waiting for him to go on.

"The tattoo on Raptor's arm – that was his name, Raptor – was for the Catbird Brotherhood. Raptor started calling me Little Big and drew me into his gang. Before long, I was running drugs for him. I felt important, and as if I belonged. But what did I know; I was a kid, just thirteen.

"Raptor would toss money at me from time to time and I would stash it away. When I had two hundred dollars I handed it to my parents, thinking they would be proud of me." Here Mike paused and his eyes began to tear up.

"They were angry. So angry. They'd had no idea what I'd been doing.

"A few months after that, Raptor took me into Mr. V.'s with him. The old man refused to serve him; said he was corrupt. Then he told me if ever I needed help, he would be there for me. Raptor was furious, swept his arm across the counter, shoving things aside, and grabbed Mr. V. He told him he'd better watch his back, 'cause he would be coming for him.

"I was scared. Then a few days later I was even more scared when I found out Mr. V.'s store had been trashed and the old man was in hospital."

Mike sipped at his chocolate again, and I noticed his hand shake.

"Anyway, it took me five years to break from the Brotherhood, and this," he raised his tattooed arm, "is all I have left to remind me what a fool I was."

"But what about your parents?" I asked.

He shook his head. "I was too ashamed of the life I'd been living to approach them. I joined the Marines and started fresh."

"Surely now is different?"

"My dad told me then that I was no longer his son. I doubt that has changed."

I was about to say something more when Mike rose and announced he was tired. Biting the words back I jumped up and put my arms round him. At first he stiffened, then relaxed and gave me a brotherly pat on the back.

"Goodnight, Polly."
"'Night, Mike."

Twenty

It felt good to get back to my little home. I opened the door and the dogs barreled past me, rushing around and sniffing at everything to make sure all was in order. While they did their doggie thing I lugged the cats inside in their carriers, and released them from incarceration. Leif and Ollie immediately rushed away, but Ditto's attention went to the dogs who were whining and pawing at the pantry door.

Uh oh. Did something go bad in there?

I pulled the door outward. There was something bad in there alright. It was Sadie, attorney Newton Alden's assistant – and she was holding a gun, pointed right at me.

Of course, the dogs rushed right in, tails wagging, excited to find a friend in the pantry of all places. But Sadie was no dog lover. She turned her gun toward Angel.

"Get them off me or they're dead."

"Angel, Vinny, Coco!" I used my sternest voice and clapped my hands. As expected, none of them paid the slightest bit of attention to me.

Horrified, I watched as Sadie's finger appeared to tighten on the trigger, when she let out a shriek and her face took on a wide-eyed look of fear. Her hands jerked upwards and at that moment the gun went off, blasting a hole through the roof of my pantry. Angel whipped around, her paws frantically scrabbling for a hold on the tile floor. With Vinny and Coco close behind, she tore through the pet door into the back yard and to safety.

"What kind of freak place is this?" Sadie screamed and kicked out viciously at Ditto. I realized instantly what had happened. Wanting attention as much as the dogs, Ditto had rubbed himself around Sadie's legs. Obviously, she didn't like cats any more than dogs.

Fortunately for my chubby feline, he was still very light on his paws and dodged the kick with impressive ease. Not one to take a threat lightly, though, he managed to shred his claws down the offending leg before he, too, vanished with speed.

That left me alone, facing a dangerously freaked-out woman with a loaded gun. I held my hands up and tried to appear non-threatening. "Sadie," I said, hoping my tone was soothing. "What do you want? How can I help you?"

"Help? You?" Her voice seemed to have gone up an octave or so. "Look what your disgusting creatures have done to me?"

She held out her bleeding limb.

"I'm so sorry, Sadie. Let me put something on that for you." If I could work my way to the kitchen, I might at least be able to grab a knife to defend myself with.

"Forget it," her lip curled in an ugly snarl. "Just get me the papers."

What? "What papers would that be, Sadie?"

"You know, the papers from Naomi Ledbetter."

"You have all the papers I have. In fact, you gave me all the papers I have."

"Stop procrastinating. Just give me the stock certificates or bonds the old witch left. I know she had money; she kept hinting about it but would never tell me where she'd hidden it, but I heard the other day you'd found it. So hand it over."

"Sadie, there are no stocks and bonds. The money is in the value of the door panel."

"What are you talking about?" She was waving that wretched gun all over the place and I could see a vein pulsing in her neck. Her eyes narrowed. "You're trying to confuse me because I've been awake for more than twenty-four hours. Well, it won't work."

My brain suddenly jerked into life. "Is that how long you've been here?"

"Of course it is, you idiot, and I've waited long enough."

Good grief. She must have heard the rumor I originally started and assumed the money was in paper. Then she'd been lying in wait for me and hadn't heard about the antique panel.

"Sadie, an antique door panel was attached to the back of a credenza. It's been valued at fifty to seventy-five thousand dollars and has already been taken away. Even if I could get to it, it's not something you can easily hide, or sell for that matter."

Sadie's color turned from an ugly red to paper white. Her body went rigid except for the arm with the gun, which began to rise in my direction. I dove for the floor, sliding under the table, and had a moment of déjà vu

about exploding eggs before I heard a shot and everything
went black.

Twenty-One

It was an evening of celebration. Earlier in the day the antique panel had sold at auction for a whopping eighty-three thousand dollars. When the auction house heard what the money was to be used for, they had waived their fee, so Welcome Home would receive the full amount. All the residents and a lot of friends were crowded into the farmhouse enjoying a big feast with much laughing and back-slapping and hugging.

I was over the moon, even though my head still hurt a little from whacking the table leg and knocking myself out as I slid across my kitchen floor. The shot I'd heard hadn't been from Sadie's gun, but was Tyler.

I'd left Angel's favorite squeaky toy, Itt - so named because it reminded me of Cousin Itt in the Adams Family - behind when I headed home. Tyler, who left soon after me, had seen it and decided to drop by my place so Angel wouldn't fuss. He'd pulled in as Sadie's gun went off in the pantry. Fortunately, *he's* able to recognize the difference between actual gunfire and exploding eggs, and crept up to the window to see what was going on.

Not wanting to spook Sadie, he grabbed the gun he keeps in his car, climbed the fence into the backyard, and peeked in through the pet door in time to see Sadie lose her cool. As she lifted her gun arm, he got a shot off and into her butt; a fairly substantial target, I might add. By the time

I came around a few minutes later, the cops and medics were arriving. Tyler had my head cradled in his arm. "The one time I don't check your house is when you get yourself in trouble." That's my knight in shining armor.

"Where's Tyler?" Mike parked himself on the arm of the chair in which I was sitting.

"He called a few minutes ago to say he's almost here."

At that moment the man of my dreams appeared in the doorway. With all the chatter I hadn't heard his car pull up. I waved to get his attention and said to Mike, "Talk of the devil."

Mike stood. "I'll leave you two alone."

I grabbed his sleeve. "No, you need to stay."

His brows drew together in puzzlement, then we both watched as Tyler made his way across the room, closely followed by a Latino man and woman. As they got close, Tyler stepped aside. The man stopped and stood stiffly, but the woman barely hesitated. Crying out in her native tongue she rushed at Mike, throwing her arms around him and sobbing on his shoulder.

Quietly, I eased myself from the chair and, joining Tyler, we left them to it. When we looked back, Mike's dad – you guessed it was his parents, right? – had inserted himself into the mix and the three of them looked like they would be a family again.

Twenty-Two

Tyler and I were sitting on the front porch in the swing as the last of the guests headed home. We were staying to help clean up but decided first to take a little time to ourselves.

"I enjoyed spending time with Mat and Jake as friends," I said. "They're so serious when they're working."

"You didn't get jealous when they both hugged me, did you?"

I looked at the grin on Tyler's face and slapped him on the chest. "Ha ha."

He wrapped his hand around mine and we sat in companiable silence for a while 'til he spoke. "I didn't get a chance to talk to the Sheriff at all. Did you find out anything?"

"Yeah. Sadie pretty much fessed up to everything. Whenever Miss Ledbetter needed to sign anything or have something notarized, Sadie would go to her house, where the old woman would drop hints about having hidden wealth.

"Remember that company that tried to get you to let them clear the furniture out of the house after Miss L. died? Sadie hired them. She thought there would be a secret drawer or some such thing where the clue to the money would be hidden. When that didn't work out she found

Delbert Fannin, private investigator, and hired him to search for the money."

"I don't get it. Why would she kill him, then?"

"She spun Del a yarn about the money being rightfully hers. Said she was related to Miss L., and that I'd coerced her into changing her will. Whether Del really believed her story or not, at the end he turned out to be a good guy and told Sadie he was going to find the money and then figure out who it really belonged to.

"Sadie hightailed it out to the farmhouse that night to conduct her search and just happened upon Del. They had an argument and she grabbed a stick and clobbered him over the head, then dragged the body under the tarp."

Tyler sighed heavily. "Del didn't deserve this. Sadie is greedy and vicious. She would have been making decent money as a legal assistant; apparently it just wasn't enough. I hope she goes away for life, especially after she tried to kill you."

"She was a shopaholic, according to Wisniewski."

Tyler guffawed.

"No, seriously," I went on. "She had a serious shopping addiction; there were piles of unopened boxes in her home, from Amazon and other online stores, and she had a mountain of debt."

"How does this happen to people?"

"Couldn't tell you. Just be glad I'm not like that; your money is safe with me." I poked Tyler playfully in the ribs. "Oh, there is some great news!"

Tyler looked at me expectantly.

"Mat and Jake are adopting Jack. They think he has great potential as a guard dog."

"That crazy pup?"

"He just needs a chance. And if anyone can give it to him, the K-9 Security guys can."

Tyler smiled. "Yep, that is good news."

It was time to head inside and do our part in the cleaning. Entering the kitchen, we bumped into Mike, Polly on his arm.

"There you are. I was looking for you," he coughed and shuffled a little. "Uh, listen. I really want to thank you both. My parents told me how you tracked them down and persuaded them to come here."

"Persuasion wasn't needed," Tyler said. "They were over-joyed to know you were safe."

"We've got a lot to make up for, and I'm going to try really hard to make them proud of me again."

I smiled. "Will you move back with them?"

Mike hesitated. "I don't know yet. Actually, I'd like to talk to you about Polly before I make any decisions."

I understood immediately. "You don't want to leave her. Well, I can tell you right now it's obvious she belongs with you, whatever you decide. She wouldn't be happy anywhere else."

A big grin spread across Mike's face, and scratching the bird's neck I said to her, "Would you, pretty girl?"

"Pretty boy, pretty boy," Polly responded, bobbing her head up and down.

"Wait a minute," Tyler frowned. "She said 'boy.' 'Pretty boy.' Is she a he?"

We all looked at each other.

Oh my gosh. "That would make sense; males are generally better talkers than females."

"But why would Naomi Ledbetter call a male parrot Polly?" Tyler asked.

"There's no way to sex a macaw by external examination," Mike chimed in. "Most people do DNA testing."

"So perhaps Miss L. thought she had a girl at first, hence the name. By the time she discovered her parrot was a boy, the name had stuck." This was exciting news to me. "Then Polly should really be Paulie, or Pally, or Phillie, or oh, oh, how about this? Polo?"

Tyler put his arm around my waist and steered me into the kitchen. Calling goodnight to Mike, to me he said, "Come on, there's work to do." But I didn't hear him. My head was still full of happy possibilities for renaming Polly the parrot.

I just love happy endings. Don't you?

If you enjoyed this story, please leave a review. Your words really mean a lot.

Get a FREE unpublished cozy mystery story and be among the first to hear about Liz's new book releases and special deals when you join her email list here:

http://lizdodwell.com/signup/

By Liz Dodwell:

Polly Parrett Pet Sitter Cozy Mysteries:
Doggone Christmas
The Christmas Kitten

Captain Finn Treasure Mysteries:
The Mystery of the One-Armed Man (Book 1)
Black Bart is Dead (Book 2)
The Gold Doubloon Mystery (Book 3)
The Game's a Foot (Book 4)
Captain Finn Boxed Set (Books 1-3)

By Liz Dodwell and Jacob Lee:

Chaplain Merriman Christian Cozy Mysteries:
Christmas Can Be Murder
Deadly Confession

Liz Dodwell devotes her time to writing and publishing from the home she shares with husband, Alex and a host of rescued dogs and cats, collectively known as "the kids." She will tell you, "I gladly suffer the luxury of working from home where I'm with my 'kids,' can toss in a load of laundry in between plotting, writing, editing and general office work while still in my PJs. I love what I do and know how lucky I am to be able to do it. Oh, and if you asked me what my hobbies are, I'd probably say reading murder mysteries, drinking champagne, romantic dinners with my husband and yodeling (just joking about that last one)."

Printed in Great Britain
by Amazon

38169011R00066